CW01214273

ii

Classic Bike Dreaming

by the same author

The Old Mechanic stories of an old motorcycle mechanic	Burringbah Books 2013
Dominator in the Shadows more stories of an old motorcycle mechanic	Amazon 2020
The Classic Bike Workshop even more stories of an old motorcycle mechanic	Amazon 2020

Classic Bike Dreaming

yet more stories of an
old motorcycle mechanic

Beautiful Jade Press

Copyright Peter J. Uren 2016

Published in Australia
by Beautiful Jade Press
Raymond Terrace, NSW 2324

National Library of Australia Cataloguing-in-Publication entry
Author: Uren, Peter, author.
Title: Classic Bike Dreaming / Peter Uren.
ISBN: 9798-69340703-9 (paperback)
Dewey Number: A823.4

First Amazon edition October 2020

This book is copyright. Apart from any fair dealing for the purpose of private study, research, criticism or review as permitted under the Copyright Act, no portion of the material contained in this publication may be reproduced by any process without the written permission of the author.

This book is a work of fiction. All characters and events are fictional and any resemblance to real people and events is purely accidental, unless otherwise indicated.

Front cover image from a Painting by Peter Kafer, commissioned by the author, photo-shopped by Glenys Tranter.
Back cover photograph taken by Glenys Tranter. Used with permission.

Contents

Chapter	Title	Page
	Prologue	1
1	A Fair Go	5
2	The Smoking Ceremony	13
3	Tell Me a Story	22
4	Safe as Houses	30
5	Two Birds with the One Stone	39
6	Good Things	47
7	The Ugly Face	56
8	Paying the Price	65
9	On the Road Again	73
10	Filial Commitments	82
11	Ghostly Appearance	90
12	Skin Deep	98
13	Haunted by His Past	106
14	Do Unto Others	114
15	Saving Grace	123
16	Living on the Edge	132
17	New Arrangements	140
18	The Reckoning	150
19	Clearing Up the Mess	160
20	Playing Santa Claus	168
	Epilogue	177

Dedication

This book is dedicated to my dear friends Dennis and Glenys Tranter, who have made a difference to the lives of many Aboriginal Australians, both in the Northern Territory where they worked for many years, as well as at home in the Hunter Region of New South Wales.

Acknowledgements

No writer ever writes in a vacuum. Even the very best have Literary Agents, Editors and Publishers, not to mention family members and friends who provide feedback on their stories and manuscripts. When I started writing for pleasure when I was still in the Australian Defence Forces, I used to farm my stories and poems out by e-mail to friends, colleagues and acquaintances. I would then wait for responses, often in vain. But I slowly developed a loyal following of readers.

Having learned how to write during my time with Defence, my stories were always very formal and read like they were reports; indeed, most of them were. It was not until I joined Stroud Writers and I started writing fictional stories, that my writing developed. I have been with them over four years now, and in that time I have written and self-published four novels, as well as numerous short stories and poems. Their ongoing critiquing of each chapter of my stories has been, and continues to be, an invaluable asset to me. But it is their friendship and loving care and support that I cherish most now.

Without a team of good editors, there would be a multitude of errors in my books, from simple spelling mistakes to poor grammar, from repetition to inconsistencies. So I would like to extend my heartfelt thanks to my dear friend, Stewart Upton, and fellow Stroud Writers, Dianne Foster and Hilary Heanly, without whom my stories would be full of errors. That is not to say that this story is perfect. Just as there are imperfections in all of us, so I had to give the "rivet counters" something to find as they pore over the story looking for some minor fault or inaccuracy. So, if you do come across something wrong, then, well done, it was placed there deliberately to give you something to discover. Now you can go back and start counting rivets again.

I would also like to thank Peter Kafer. Peter, an Aboriginal Australian and a proud Dharawahl man, has become my friend over the past couple of years. A former Police Officer, teacher and now an artist, he has provided me with invaluable guidance, encouragement and support as I have been writing. There are some things that cannot be taught from books or on the Internet. Peter has opened my eyes to some things that could only be told or experienced. He has also provided the painting for the front cover of this book. Thank you, brother.

Prologue

The Tamworth Local and District Court House is a squat, unattractive building located next to the Police Station near the centre of the city. It could be an intimidating building to the uninitiated, but for Paul Saunders, this was the sixth time that he had appeared before the local Magistrate. Dressed in his best second-hand ill-fitting St Vincent de Paul trousers, shirt and track shoes, Paul stood in the dock after his name was called. His long, normally unkempt hair had been dampened and combed back. He looked around the room in vain for a friendly face he recognised. But other than the Police Prosecutor, the Magistrate and his Lawyer, there was no-one except an old Aboriginal man whom he did not know. When instructed to do so, he sat on the chair. He felt very alone.

'Who's defending this case?' asked the Magistrate.

A fresh-faced Legal-Aid Lawyer stood, 'I am, Your Honour.'

'Thank you, Mr Ellison. What are the charges?'

The Police Prosecutor stood. 'Your Honour, the defendant is charged with: three counts of break, enter and steal; two cases of malicious damage; and one each of possession of stolen property and car theft. He is also charged with driving a motor vehicle without a licence.'

'How does the Defendant plead?'

'Not guilty, Your Honour.'

'Really Mr Ellison. I hope you're not going to waste the Court's time and my time defending the indefensible.'

'Ah, no, Your Honour.'

'Very well then, what are the facts of the case?'

The Police Prosecutor outlined the allegations against Paul; how he had been caught driving, without a current driver's licence, a vehicle that had earlier been reported stolen from East Tamworth. In the boot of the vehicle were a number of items, which he listed, that had been reported stolen from three premises in South Tamworth. In two of the premises the defendant had allegedly defecated on the floor and spread the faeces on the walls.

The Police Prosecutor then called on the two Police Constables who made the arrest to give their testimony. After each swearing to tell the whole truth and nothing but the truth, they in turn read from their notebooks the events of the night in question.

'Was anyone else in the car at the time?' asked the Magistrate.

'Yes, Your Honour. There was a juvenile who appeared in the Children's Court last month.'

'Very well, Mr Ellison, do you have any witnesses you wish to call for the Defence?'

'Just the Defendant, Your Honour.'

'Alright, let's hear what he has to say.'

Paul stood up in the Dock and gave the affirmation.

'You've heard the Police reports, now tell the Court what really happened that night,' said Paul's Legal-Aid Lawyer.

'All I done was drive a car wiffout a licence. I never knew it was nicked. I never went inta them houses, an' I never nicked anyfing. An' I never knew there was stuff in the boot what was nicked.'

'What about the Malicious Damage.'

'Yeah, I never crapped on the floor in them houses, or spread shit on the walls. That was the others what done it but.'

The Magistrate asked, 'Mr Saunders, how would you have known that the others had defecated on the floor, unless you were in the house to see it? And if you were in the house, you share in their guilt, even if, as you say, you didn't do anything or take anything. Do you have anything more to say in your own Defence?'

'Nah,' replied Paul.

'No, Your Honour,' corrected the Magistrate.

'No, Ya Honour.'

Paul sat down again.

'Do you have any other witnesses, Mr Ellison?'

'No, Your Honour.'

'Very well, Mr Saunders, please stand.'

Paul stood again.

'Paul Saunders, I find you guilty on all charges. Mr Ellison, do you have anything to add before the Defendant is sentenced?'

'Yes, Your Honour.'

The Legal-Aid Lawyer outlined the difficulties of Paul Saunders' upbringing, of his low socio-economic background, his lack of formal education, how he had been subjected to violence and abuse from a young age, and that as an Aboriginal youth, he was from one of the most marginalised groups in Australia. With support, he informed the Magistrate, Paul had good prospects for rehabilitation, and that a custodial sentence would not be appropriate for him.

The Magistrate then adjourned the court for one hour while he examined Paul's file and his long criminal history. When he returned he ordered Paul to stand.

'Paul Saunders, I recognise that you have had a difficult life, despite your tender age. However, this Court cannot condone such disgusting acts done in the homes of innocent, decent people. You have displayed a complete disregard for the property of others, and no argument can minimise your culpability. You have had several chances in the past, and you have made no effort to change your ways. You have shown no hint of remorse, and despite what Mr Ellison has said on your behalf, I see little prospects for your rehabilitation. Therefore, I sentence you to five years imprisonment, with a non-parole period of three and a half years. Do you have anything to say?'

'No, Ya Honour.'

'Take the Prisoner down.'

Chapter 1

A FAIR GO

Tamworth Correctional Centre is a medium security prison for males, situated in North Tamworth, in the New England Region of NSW. Like many such facilities in Australia, the number of inmates from an Aboriginal and Torres Strait Islander background is out of proportion to their numbers in the general population. That is not to say that members of that Community are necessarily more likely to commit a crime, but they are more likely to be sent to gaol.

Paul Saunders, of the Kamilaroi people, grew up in the suburb of Taminda, a stone's throw from the Tamworth Racecourse. He had been in and out of prison since his early teens. For the most part, his were crimes relatively minor: malicious damage; break, enter and steal; possession of stolen property; and car theft. But now into his mid-twenties, he was determined to break the cycle of crime and subsequent imprisonment; he wanted a clean break from his past.

Having left school at the earliest opportunity, Paul had little by way of formal education. Not that he was unintelligent, indeed, over the past three years he had been participating in a training program in the prison run by TAFE NSW. At the end of the month, he would be graduating near the top of his class as a qualified motorcycle mechanic. He would soon appear before the Parole Board where he hoped to be released. Both the Prison Welfare Officer and his Parole Officer had been canvassing all of the larger motorcycle workshops in the region in order to gain a placement for Paul; so far, without success.

Besides employment, the other important issue that the Prison Welfare Officer needed to resolve to allow Paul a smooth transition back into the community, was accommodation. He could go back to the family home, but all too often, released prisoners would revert to their old habits when they returned to familiar surroundings. Ideally, he would live and work away from his home and the temptations those locations brought, but there were few options, even in a city the size of Tamworth.

Michael had been operating the business, more or less on his own since Kieran's death and his father-in-law's heart attack. While the old mechanic had made an attempt at returning to work, repairing and servicing motorcycles, he was clearly struggling with his fitness. More often than not, he would arrive at the workshop out of breath from the effort of pushing his walker the short distance from his small cottage across the laneway. He would then have to sit down and rest while Michael made tea for them both.

With Katie still on Maternity Leave at home looking after baby Kieran, the old mechanic could at least assume responsibility for completing all of her administrative tasks, including accounting, preparing invoices, banking and ordering new stock as required. Even though he would have much preferred to spend his time fixing motorbikes, his task was the necessary evil of the business. But at least it freed up Michael to deal with their customers' bikes. Nevertheless, in recent days he had started to do some of the minor jobs around the workshop, while leaving the heavy lifting to his son-in-law.

As the weather improved and the warmer months approached, the business was becoming steadily busier as more and more classic motorcycle owners needed their machines fettled. Michael was quickly coming to the realisation that he would soon need someone else to help out with the increasing workload.

It was a Monday morning. The two men had just broken for their usual mid-morning smoko when a car drove slowly up the laneway outside the workshop. The two men looked at one another.

'You expecting someone?' asked Michael.

The old mechanic shook his head. 'Nuh!'

Michael rose and left his mug of tea to meet the visitor. When the occupant of the car emerged, Michael greeted him, 'G'day.'

The bearded man appeared a little older than Michael, probably in his early thirties. He was casually dressed with a nametag that read "Brian Redmond" pinned to his shirtfront.

'Good morning, are you Mr Edwards?' asked Brian, his hand extended.

Michael took the proffered hand and shook it. 'No, George Edwards is inside, I'm Mike Jones.'

The Prison Welfare Officer followed Michael into the workshop. He looked around the inside of the building before turning to where George was seated.

'Pardon me for not standing,' the old mechanic thrust out his hand to shake hands with his visitor, 'but I've not been very well. I'm George Edwards, how can I help you?'

Before Brian could introduce himself, Michael interjected, 'I've just boiled the jug, would ya like a cuppa?'

'Yeah, tah; white an' one.' Then turning to the old mechanic, Brian continued, 'I'm Brian Redmond, Welfare Officer at the Tamworth Correctional Centre, and I'm after your assistance.'

'I'm all ears,' replied the old mechanic.

'Actually, it's not me who needs your assistance; it's one of my clients.'

'You mean a prisoner.'

'Well, yeah, but hopefully, not for much longer. He's coming up for parole and we need to find him a work placement and somewhere to stay.'

'Who told you about me?'

'I've been to all the larger motorbike businesses in the district, but no-one's willing to help. They all tell me their rosters are full.'

'So you've come to me as a last resort.'

'Well, yeah.'

'Who is this guy?'

'His name's Paul Saunders and he's been doing a Motorcycle Mechanics Course at TAFE for the past three years as part of his rehabilitation.'

'What's he been locked up for?' asked Michael.

'Break, enter and steal; possession of stolen property; and car theft.'

Michael frowned and expressed a doubtful look.

'What's he like?' continued the old mechanic.

'He's a good worker, by all reports, and he'll be graduating near the top of his class. He just needs someone to give him a job.'

'Does he have a bike licence?'

'Not yet, but he's booked in for a test as soon as he's released.'

'Well, that's not much use to me. I need someone who can test ride the bikes we repair.'

Michael jumped in again. 'If he's a good mechanic as you say, I can do the test rides for both of us. And besides, most of the bikes we work on are LAMS approved anyway, so he'll be able to ride them, even on a Provisional Licence. And it's not as if we don't need another mechanic to work here.'

'Hmm, I don't know,' agonised the old mechanic. 'Honesty's really important in our game. If he's got experience stealing, who's to say he won't do it again?'

'I've spoken with Paul on several occasions over the past few months. He's a nice young guy who's really determined to make a break with his past. Yeah, he was busted, but he's paid his dues. He just wants someone to give him a second chance.'

'Where's he gonna stay. If he doesn't have a licence, I'm guessing he doesn't have any transport either.'

'Yeah, that's another matter I need to resolve.'

'There's always the bus,' suggested Michael eagerly, 'or I could give him a lift, if he doesn't live too far away.'

'Don't get too far ahead o' yourself, I haven't said yes yet,' cautioned the old mechanic. 'I wanna meet him first, and have a talk. Can you organise that?'

'Yeah, I can probably arrange it for this afternoon, if that's convenient?'

'What about me? I've gotta work with him; I'd like ta meet him too,' said Michael.

'You can meet him, if and when he starts,' advised the old mechanic. 'Besides, someone's gotta do the work 'round here.' Then, addressing Brian he continued, 'Are you gonna pick me up and bring me back?'

'Yeah, I can do that. What's say I come back around one?'

'I'll be ready.'

Brian returned just after 1:00 pm. On the way into Tamworth, the old mechanic struck up a conversation.

'How long have you worked in the prison system?'

'After I graduated from UNE, I worked casually for the Health Department for a coupla years. Then this job came up and I applied for it. I've been with 'em seven years now.'

'Wha' didja study at Uni?'

'Social Work.'

'Do you like working in the prison?'

'It has its challenges, like all jobs. It's good when you see young blokes like Paul turn their lives around, and make a positive contribution to society.'

'I suppose you see your fair share of returnees.'

'Yeah, for some blokes, the only stability they have in their lives is the prison. They get three cooked meals, a roof over their heads, hot and cold showers and clean clothes. Someone tells them when ta get up and when to go ta bed. Those who live on the streets on the outside are sometimes better off in gaol.'

It is a different world to the one I live in, the old mechanic mused.

Brian pulled into the prison carpark. He unloaded the old mechanic's walker from the boot and led him slowly to reception. Once inside, he signed the Visitor's Register, underwent a search and filled out a questionnaire. He felt the whole process quite intimidating.

When they finally entered the prison proper, the old mechanic asked, 'Do all visitors hafta go through this rigmarole?'

'Yep, everyone. But you were lucky, if the guards suspected you were carrying contraband, they could've ordered a strip search.'

'How often do they catch people tryin' ta smuggle stuff in?'

'Every week.'

'What happens to 'em?'

'They get charged, and often end up inside as well.'

The old mechanic followed Brian into an office with large reinforced glass windows in the wall and door. Inside were a table and three chairs. On the table was a file with Paul Saunders' name on the front cover. Inside were his academic records and reports. The two men sat down on one side of the table.

'Have a look through his file if you like; there're all his test results from his course. Paul'll be here soon.'

'I'm not really interested in results; anyone c'n study for a test. I'm more interested in his attitude.'

After a few minutes, Paul was ushered into the room by one of the prison guards. He was of medium height, thin build, a dark complexion, heavy brow and flattened nose. His eyes were almost black, his teeth a brilliant white and he was clean shaven. A mop of dark brown unkempt hair covered his head.

The old mechanic turned to Brian. 'You didn't tell me he was an Aborigine.'

'That's all right Boss, he didn't tell me you was a white fella,' replied Paul quickly, flashing a wide smile.

'What does it matter?' responded Brian. 'Black, white or brindle, it's not the colour of your skin that matters, but whether you can do the job.'

'Can you do the job?' asked the old mechanic.

'Boss, I been fixin' bikes an' cars since I was a little tacker.'

'The bikes we fix are classic British motorcycles: BSAs, Nortons, and Triumphs mostly. I doubt you've even seen one before.'

'Boss, a bike, is a bike, is a bike. It's got two wheels, a frame an' a motor. What I don't know, I can learn. All I need's a fair go but.'

The old mechanic paused for a few moments. 'You've got some spunk, that's for sure. Alright, let me think about it. I need to talk with the others first. But one thing: don't call me Boss; me name's George.'

'Alright, thanks George.'

The two men shook hands.

'The thing I need to know,' continued the old mechanic, 'is can I trust you?'

'Trust me to do what? To fix bikes? Sure, you c'n trust me.'

'No, I don't doubt you can do the job. What I want to know is, can I trust you?'

Now it was Paul's turn to pause. At last he looked deep into the old mechanic's eyes. 'Yes, George, you c'n trust me.'

TAFE – Technical & Further Education
LAMS – Learner Approved Motorcycle Scheme
UNE – University New England, Armidale

Chapter 2

THE SMOKING CEREMONY

The old mechanic was in two minds as he returned to the workshop. Like many of his generation, he had grown up with certain beliefs and opinions about the indigenous population of Australia, and not all of them positive. He did not consider himself to be a racist as such, preferring to judge people by their character, rather than the colour of their skin, but the few Aborigines that he knew seemed to have, in his opinion, a proverbial chip on each of their shoulders. Although, he had to admit, he too would probably feel resentment if others hated him just because of his race and who he was descended from.

Michael was working on a Norton Commando when the old mechanic wheeled his walker back into the workshop.

'How'd you go at the prison?' asked Michael. 'Are you gonna offer him a job?'

'I thought I'd talk to you and Katie about it first. You know he's an Aborigine.'

Michael stopped what he was doing and looked across at his father-in-law who was now seated on his walker. 'So? Is that a problem?'

'Well, not for me, but I'm not the one who's gonna be working closely with him.'

'I'm more concerned about whether he can do the job, than who he's related to or his skin colour.'

'I just hope we don't end up regretting it.'

'George, when Kieran started workin' here, you had misgivings. But by the time he'd completed his probationary period, you were more than happy to make him permanent. If this guy … what's his name again?'

'Paul.'

'If Paul doesn't work out after three months, give him the flick. But good mechanics aren't exactly linin' up to work here. We prob'ly need him as much as he needs us.'

'Yeah, I s'pose so. Oh, one thing I did pick up on; he gives as good as he takes.'

'How so?'

'Well, when he entered the room, I said to Brian, "You didn't tell me he was an Aborigine." Then, quick as a flash Paul responded, "That's all right Boss; he didn't tell me you were a white fella."'

Michael laughed.

'Do you think we should run it past Katie?'

'I can tell her tonight when I get home, but I don't think it'll be a problem. When do you need to let Brian know?'

'By noon tomorrow.'

'When will he start?'

'I should find out then.'

As Michael had expected, Katie had no qualms about an Aboriginal mechanic coming to work in the business. She was more concerned that he had spent time in prison. However, she was pleased that someone had finally been identified to help Michael with his heavy workload.

In anticipation of his being granted parole, work-release was approved for Paul during the final months of his sentence. This arrangement suited the old mechanic and Michael as it allowed a period of "getting to know one another" before he became a fulltime employee, and it would give them both a chance to see whether Paul would fit into the team. The Toyota Hi Ace prison van would be dropping the inmates at their various locations around Tamworth. This meant that Paul's hours would be dictated by the prison van's arrival rather than by his employer.

With social housing in high demand in the region, Brian was having difficulty in securing suitable alternate accommodation for Paul. The only short-term emergency accommodation was a men's refuge, which was patently unsuitable. It seemed, therefore, that he would have to return to his family's residence in Taminda, unless something better could be arranged.

The old mechanic and Michael were already in the workshop servicing two of their customers' motorcycles when the prison van arrived the following Monday morning. Brian was aboard to act as both guide to the van driver, and to introduce the prison inmate to his new surrounds. Michael left the motorcycle he was working on to meet the van.

'Morning Brian,' he called when the Welfare Officer had climbed from the front passenger seat.

'Hello Mike.' Brian turned to pull the rear door open, allowing one of the passengers to alight. 'This here's Paul, Paul Saunders. Paul, this is Mike Jones; I believe you'll be working for him.'

The two men shook hands. 'I thought I'd be workin' fer George but,' said Paul shyly.

'George handed the reins over to me, so I'm in charge now. Come on, George's inside.' Turning to Brian, he asked, 'When'll you be back to pick him up?'

'Four-ish.'

'Okay, see you then.'

The old mechanic had some forms for Paul to complete, before Michael gave him a tour of the workshop and the safety briefing. It was mid-morning before they were ready to start work and for the new mechanic to show his employers what he was capable of, but not before they had their morning smoko.

Like Kieran before him, Paul preferred coffee over tea. 'I like me coffee like me women, strong, sweet and black: two teaspoons of coffee and three sugars.'

The other two mechanics shuddered at the thought of what that concoction would taste like.

Once all three men were comfortably seated with their brew of choice, Paul asked, 'Who's Kieran?'

'He was your predecessor,' replied the old mechanic. 'He had a bad riding accident a couple of months back and passed away. That's his bike over there under the tarp.'

'Did you have an accident too?'

'No, why do you ask?'

'Well, you usin' that walker to get about.'

The old mechanic laughed. 'No, I had a heart attack a few weeks after Kieran's crash.'

'Ah, that's not good, two bad things happenin' together.

'Actually,' cut in Michael, 'it was three things. Just after Kieran's death, Katie, my missus, gave birth prematurely.'

'Is she okay?'

'Yeah, she's fine.'

'And the baby?'

'Yeah he's good now. Anyway, it's time to get to work. The Triumph T100 Tiger needs a service Paul, so you can show us what you're capable of.'

By the end of the day, Paul's head was spinning, as he tried to take in all the information. Everything was so different compared to the prison workshop. Despite his assertion at the interview with the old mechanic, most of the bikes he had worked on in gaol were late model Japanese two and four stroke single cylinder dirt bikes. While he had studied the theory of overhead valve pushrod engines and points ignition, he had only ever worked on overhead camshaft engines with electronic ignition. At least he knew how to adjust tappets and tune twin carburettors, even if the carbies were Mikunis rather than Amals.

Growing up as a teenager, Paul had little time for his Aboriginal culture. Sure, he had heard the dreaming stories that had been passed down from his ancestors, but they seemed to have little relevance for him. It was not until he underwent the initiation ceremony whilst in the prison, and so became a man, that his culture started to make sense and so have greater importance for him. And it was his culture that he had to thank for giving him the motivation to improve himself and to make a break with his criminal past.

The issue playing on Paul's mind as he returned to the prison later that afternoon had nothing to do with fixing classic British motorcycles. Rather, it has the run of catastrophic mishaps that had occurred to three of the four people who worked in the business. So he was determined that he would need to speak with one of the Elders of his mob at the earliest opportunity about what should be done.

Uncle Danny Stewart was a prominent member of the Aboriginal and Torres Straight Islander Community in Tamworth and an Elder of the Kamilaroi people. He also happened to be a regular visitor to the Tamworth Correctional Centre. During one of his weekend visits, Paul asked to see him. In the same room where he had met the old mechanic, he was ushered in to see Uncle Danny.

'Hello Paulie, I hear you is comin' up for release soon. Your mama, she's gonna be so happy to have her baby comin' home.'

'Hello Uncle Danny. Thanks for comin' to see me. I need your help.'

'Is you in trouble ag'in?'

'No Uncle Danny, it's the people givin' me a job might be in trouble but.'

'Wha' daya mean?'

Paul related the succession of events that occurred to Kieran, Katie and the old mechanic over a short period of time. He then explained that Kieran's damaged motorcycle was now parked in the workshop.

'Was this crashed motorbike in the workshop when the new baby comes an' the old fella has his heart problems?' asked Uncle Danny.

'Yeah, I think so,' replied Paul.

'Hmm. I think we needs to clean the workshop of the evil spirits.'

'That's what I was thinkin'. Can you organise it?'

'Yeah, I can, but don'cha think you should talk to them white fellas first; they might not like us doin' somethin' like this.'

'Yeah, I'll talk to 'em on Mond'y.'

Paul was much happier now that the Kamilaroi Elder was onboard to cleanse the workshop. He only hoped that the old mechanic and Michael were prepared to allow the ceremony to take place. Some white fellas were suspicious of Aboriginal culture and lore, and indifferent to the harm evil spirits could do. He just hoped they would see things from his perspective.

The prison van dropped him off at the workshop on Monday morning just after 8:00 am, but it was not until the men took their mid-morning break that Paul raised the subject.

'In our culture, when there's a series of bad things happenin', we believe a evil spirit might be the cause.'

The old mechanic, who had a Christian upbringing, was sceptical and instantly dismissive of any thought of spirits, evil or otherwise. 'I don't believe any of that crap.'

'There has to be a cause for what happened,' said Michael. 'You said yourself that bad things come in threes. Whether it's bad luck or bad omens, who's to say there aren't such things as evil spirits.' He turned back to Paul, 'Can you do something about it?'

'I was speakin' to one of the Elders of me tribe on the weekend, and he agreed wiff me that it might be an evil spirit. If you're okay about it, he'd be happy to come an' have a smokin' ceremony to clean the workshop.'

'And what if we're not okay?' asked the old mechanic.

'Them evil spirits might make somethin' else bad happen but.'

'Come on George,' pleaded Michael, 'what's the worst that could happen? So, the workshop fills up with smoke. But imagine what might happen if there really is an evil spirit in here; what's the next disaster that could eventuate.'

The old mechanic was surprised at Michael's enthusiastic defence of Paul's position. 'Look, at the end of the day, I don't really care wha'cha do Mike, if it makes you happy, just as long as you don't burn the place down. And besides, you're in charge, do wha'cha like, just don't expect me to be a part of it.'

Michael was pleased with his small win. He turned to Paul. 'When can this Elder friend of yours perform the smokin' ceremony?'

'He wanted me to check wiff you first. Is tomorrow awright?'

Michael turned to the old mechanic.

'Don't look at me Mike, I don't care, remember.'

Michael turned back to Paul. 'Yeah, tomorrow's fine. Make it as early as you can.'

'I'll get Uncle Danny to meet me here when the van arrives in the morning. Can I use the phone ta call him?'

'Sure.'

Uncle Danny Stewart arrived at the workshop just after 7:30 am driving an old Holden Commodore station wagon. Michael met him as he emerged from his car.

'Hello Mr Stewart, I'm Mike Jones, Paul hasn't arrived yet.'

'G'day Mike.' The two men shook hands. 'Everyone calls me Uncle Danny.'

'Okay, Uncle Danny.'

The Kamilaroi Elder opened the back of the station wagon and retrieved a number of items including a pair of clapping sticks, a coolamon, several leafy branches from the Emu Bush, some dry bark kindling and his fire sticks. He placed all the items on the ground inside the door of the workshop before turning his attention to Michael.

'Where's this modabike that killed your friend?'

'I'll introduce you to my father-in-law first.'

After the introductions, Michael led the Elder to the Triumph Bonneville hiding under a tarp in a corner of the workshop. He reacted by throwing up his hands when the motorcycle was revealed.

'Whoa, this bike has powerful bad spirits. Him killed more 'an one fella.'

Meanwhile, Paul had arrived in the prison van. He entered the workshop in time to hear Uncle Danny's words.

'Can you do somethin' about it Uncle Danny?'

'Yeah, I think so.'

About this time, Katie arrived with baby Kieran. Like Michael, she was more open to indigenous culture, and was curious to learn what was involved in a smoking ceremony. The pair had heard of the ceremony and seen snippets on the television, but had never understood what was involved.

Uncle Danny stripped down to his trousers, and Paul to his shorts, and daubed themselves with white ochre, before the Kamilaroi Elder created fire in the coolamon with his sticks. When the kindling was alight, he added the Emu Bush branches, producing clouds of white smoke. Once he was satisfied, the ceremony could begin.

Paul took up the pair of sticks and started tapping a beat and singing as Uncle Danny took the coolamon and waved the smoke around the inside of the workshop, as well as over and around the motorcycle. In no time, the air was thick with the acrid white smoke.

When he believed that the building and the Triumph had been cleansed of the evil spirits, he invited those interested to pass through the smoke to cleanse themselves. Michael and Katie, with baby Kieran in her arms, joined Paul in walking through the smoke. Despite his scepticism, even the old mechanic joined in with the others. To ensure the evil spirit did not return, Paul made a line of ochre around the outside walls of the workshop.

Chapter 3

TELL ME A STORY

After the smoking ceremony had concluded, Uncle Danny was invited to stay and have morning tea with the small group. Unlike Paul, he had tea, but in like fashion with the younger man, his was strong, sweet and black. Katie had made some Anzac biscuits which were shared around.

Once everyone was settled, Michael asked the Kamilaroi Elder, 'Where did you learn about the smokin' ceremony an' evil spirits?'

'The dreamin' stories was passed down from the ancestors. When we was little, the ol' men would take us out bush and tell us the stories 'round the camp fire.'

'We used to do the same,' broke in the old mechanic. 'Only we were in the Boy Scouts and we used to go campin' an' we'd tell ghost stories round the camp fire.'

'You never told any to me,' accused Katie.

'That's 'cos you're a girl. Scary ghost stories were only fer boys.'

Katie gave a hurt look, so her father continued, 'And besides, by the time you came along, I'd forgotten 'em all.'

Although not entirely convinced, Katie turned to Uncle Danny, 'Can you tell us some dreaming stories, please?'

Michael jumped in. 'Umm, actually, we've got work to do.'

'Yes, but I haven't,' argued Katie.

'I need ta be goin' but,' advised Uncle Danny. 'Maybe next time I c'n tell you 'bout Gawarrgay, the great Emu in the Sky.'

Katie knew there would likely not be a "next time" but she readily agreed all the same. After all she thought, while ever Paul was working there, Uncle Danny might just make another visit, although she hoped it was not to scare off any more evil spirits.

When the Kamilaroi Elder had gone and the two younger mechanics had resumed servicing the assortment of classic motorcycles that were in the workshop, Katie turned to her father, 'Why do people tell stories? Why don't they just write them down in books?'

'Not everyone c'n write Sweetheart, or read for that matter. In fact, Aboriginal Australians didn't even have a written language before the white man arrived on the scene. The only way to pass on stories was to memorise them and tell them to the next generation. And besides a story told is far better than one that's read. When you were little you used to love it when I told you stories – I didn't just read them, I acted them out. It didn't matter how many times you'd heard *Goldilocks and the Three Bears*, *Little Red Riding Hood* or *Snow White and the Seven Dwarves*, you just loved 'em to death.'

Katie smiled at the thought, 'Yeah, I remember. You know I've still got that old book of fairy tales at home.'

'You'd do well to bring those old stories to life for young Kieran when he gets older. He'll thank you for it when he grows up.'

'I'd much prefer to tell him stories of the Dreamtime.'

Baby Kieran, who to this point had been asleep in his carry basket in the office, announced that he was awake by crying, and that it was mealtime. Katie, who was still breastfeeding, closed the office door while she fed him. After feeding him and changing his nappy, it was time for them to return home.

As she was leaving, Paul called out, 'Hey missus, I c'n tell ya a dreamin' story if ya like; I know some of 'em too.'

'It'll have to be at lunchtime,' advised Michael, 'we've got plenty of work to do.'

'Okay, but it can't be today,' replied Katie. 'How about tomorrow?'

'I'll be here, I hope.'

Paul was beginning to feel that he was fitting in with the others in the workshop. While the old mechanic still regarded him with a degree of wariness, Michael had made him feel that he was an important part of the team. He appreciated the fact that they were only a small workforce and that his supervisor was very patient with him. Even though he was a fully qualified motorcycle mechanic, he realised that he still had a lot to learn when it came to maintaining classic British motorbikes.

Although he was still technically an inmate of Tamworth Correctional Centre, during working hours Paul started to feel more and more as if he had already been released. It was only when the prison van arrived and he would be driven back and locked up again that he was reminded that he still had time to serve, albeit weeks rather than months or years.

Some of the longer-term inmates had begun to put pressure on him to smuggle in contraband like cigarettes, drugs, mobile phones, SIM cards or pornographic material. Paul was not really in a position to point-blank refuse these demands; however, he did point out that he was subject to searches, the same as everyone else, and so any banned items would likely be confiscated and he would be charged. And besides, he told them, he was not prepared to do anything that might jeopardise his impending release.

One of the conditions of his work-release was that Paul was to remain within the confines of the workshop while ever he was out of the prison. The upshot was that Michael could not ask him to collect the lunches from the sandwich shop. With Katie still on leave and the old mechanic still not fit enough to walk long distances, this meant that Michael had to make the journey himself, whether or not he was busy. His return signalled that it was time for lunch.

When the three men had settled down to eat, Paul asked Michael, 'Where'd ya learn how to fix all them old motorbikes? They don't teach this stuff at TAFE.'

'I did me apprenticeship here. George taught me everything I needed to know, and then some.'

'Why don't we work on newer bikes?'

The old mechanic jumped in. 'That because every other bike shop in Tamworth looks after more modern machinery, leaving the old stuff for us. Everyone in the district who owns a classic British motorcycle knows that we can look after their bike for them.'

'Who looks after old Jap bikes?'

The question hung in the air, with neither Michael nor the old mechanic seemingly willing to answer. Eventually the old mechanic responded, 'There aren't that many classic Japanese bikes, not compared to classic British motorcycles. The same as there aren't that many Italian bikes, or German or French. If we were to specialise in old Jap bikes there probably wouldn't be enough work in Tamworth to make it worthwhile.'

'And besides,' added Michael, 'the thing that keeps our business going is the availability of spare parts. We can get almost any part for any British motorcycle made after World War 2. The same can't be said of spare parts for old Japanese bikes. And even if we could get the parts, they're usually a lot more expensive by comparison.'

'Aren't Japanese bikes more reliable but,' suggested Paul, 'and don't break down as often.'

The old mechanic smiled. 'If motorcycles didn't break down, there wouldn't be any work for us to do. Having said that, even the most reliable motorcycle still needs to be maintained, and parts still wear out. In my experience, British made parts don't wear out any quicker than Japanese made. Not only that, but a lot of spares these days are made in China, India or Thailand.'

'Speaking of having work to do,' interrupted Michael.

The afternoon passed quickly. Before he realised it, the prison van's horn was tooting, indicating that it was time for Paul to leave.

'I'll see youse tomorrow,' he yelled as he made his way quickly to the waiting vehicle.

'Make sure you've got a story for Katie,' called Michael, 'she'll be expectin' you ta tell her somethin' at lunchtime.'

The van pulled up inside the prison walls. Only after the gates were shut behind the vehicle were the prisoners allowed out. They were each then individually searched before being allowed inside. The vehicle was also searched before being parked.

It was already mealtime, so the prisoners had no time to return to their shared cells before they lined up to be served their meals. Paul was in the middle of a queue of about 80 men of various ages. Some had been in prison for a long time, while others were still relatively new.

Suddenly there was a commotion near the end of the line. A middle-aged man, who he recognised as one of those on work-release, had collapsed on the floor, his hands covering his midriff. Another prisoner, whom Paul knew to be in for murder, was standing over him in a threatening stance. It was this second man who had wanted Paul to smuggle drugs into the prison. Paul guessed that the other man had also been "asked". A pair of guards quickly appeared and escorted the murderer away. No-one helped the middle-aged man to his feet. In the prison, it was every man for himself.

Paul grabbed his meal and made his way to a table that had a spare seat. While most things were shared by the different nationalities within the prison, meal tables were definitely not, at least not if you wanted to eat in peace. Aboriginals ate with other Aboriginals, Vietnamese ate with other Vietnamese, Lebanese with other Lebanese, and so on. Those who sat at Paul's table were other members of the Kamilaroi mob.

'How was your day, Paulie?' asked one of the older members at his table.

'Good thanks Uncle. I'm learning new stuff every day.'

'Are those white fellas treatin' you good?'

'Yeah, pretty much. I'm not sure the old fella's really that keen on me bein' there. Me boss seems pretty happy with me but.'

'They gonna give you a job when you get out?'

'Dunno yet Uncle, I hope so but. If it was up to me boss, Michael, I fink he'd give me a job.'

'Good! We don't wanna see you back inside here any time soon.'

'That makes two of us, Uncle. I've still gotta find somewhere to stay but. If I go back 'ome, I'm pretty sure me ol' friends'll want me to go right back robbin' and stealin' with 'em again.'

'Where ya gonna live if ya don't go back home?' asked one of the others at the table. 'Everyone's expectin' ya to go back to livin' with ya family.'

'Yeah, that's the trouble.'

Paul went to sleep that night thinking about where he could live on his release. Every alternative he could think of had a negative connotation associated with it.

Most of the prison population was awakened by an alarm at 6:00 am. This gave everyone the time to complete their ablutions before breakfast at 7:00. However, those on work-release had to leave the prison at 7:00 am, so they were woken at 5:00 with breakfast at 6:00.

The cell was still dark when Paul was shaken awake. The prison was quiet; the only sounds were the snores of his sleeping fellow prisoners. In the distance he could hear the unmistakable sound of a kookaburra. He smiled as he remembered the dreaming story he was once told by one of the older men of his mob.

The two mechanics were very busy throughout the entire morning, servicing and repairing a variety of classic British motorcycles belonging to their customers. They only realised that it was lunchtime when Katie arrived, together with baby Kieran.

'I hope you've got a story ready to tell me Paul,' she called as she swept into the workshop.

'Sure do, missus.'

When everyone was seated with their lunches, Paul began. 'This here's **my** story about why the kookaburra can be heard callin' in the mornin'. One day, a long, long time ago, there was a Good Spirit who lived up in the sky. When he flew high above the red earth, he saw how beautiful it was when it was lit up by the brightness of his fire. So, he thought to himself that he would make a blazin' fire every day, and so he did. He called the blazin' fire the Sun.

'Every night, the Good Spirit and all his spirit helpers would collect wood for the fire. They would heap it up until the pile of wood was big enough. Then they would send out the Mornin' Star to warn everyone on the earth that the fire would soon be lit. However, the Good Spirit soon re'lised that this warnin' from the Mornin' Star wasn't bright enough to wake everyone up; there was a big mob who slept right through the great display.

'All the spirits gathered together to talk about their problem. Some said this, an' some said that. Event'ally they decided that, instead of a small light, it'd be better to find someone who'd be able ta make a great noise before the dawn to wake up everyone who was sleepin' to announce the comin' of the Sun. So, they asked the Goo-Koor-gaka, to broadcast the comin' of the Sun every mornin' to wake the sleepers. We know him as the kookaburra, and that's why you c'n hear him callin' in the mornin' announcin' it'll soon be sunrise.'

Chapter 4

SAFE AS HOUSES

Paul's time was dual paced: his days in the workshop passed quickly enough, but the nights and weekends spent in the prison dragged by slowly. The weekends were the worst, especially if he did not have any visitors – Paul had not had any for over two months. Uncle Danny Stewart had passed a message to him via the Prison Welfare Officer that his mother had been unwell, which was a euphemism he had used in the past when she had been drinking.

Paul loved his mother, but he hated when she would be on the grog, which sadly, was most of the time. She always drank to excess with her latest "fella" who, on occasions, would become violent with her, or with him and his siblings. On more than one occasion his mother had ended up in hospital after being beaten up by her drinking partner.

Paul did not know his real father. His mother either did not know who he was, or just would not tell him; he suspected the latter. There had been a string of men over the years, but there had been no-one who had been around long enough to fulfil the role of a father to him. The outcome was that, in his early teen years, he had fallen in with the "wrong" crowd. The gang he joined were mostly Aboriginal youths about the same age as Paul who spent their time honing their skills in house breaking and car stealing. The gang leader was an older fella by the name of Vince or Vinnie.

If he returned to reside in the family home, the chances were high that he would revert to his old way of life; the pressure on him to run with the gang would be just too great. So, by all possible lawful means, he was determined not to go back to living with his family. But his options were limited, and time was fast running out. The Parole Board had already approved Paul's release subject to him finding suitable accommodation. He only had one more week of his sentence to serve.

The three mechanics sat down for their mid-morning break; Paul sipping his coffee while the others drank their tea.

After a period of silence, Paul spoke. 'The Parole Board's lettin' me out nex' Mond'y – at long last.'

The old mechanic looked up from his mug. 'You don't sound very excited. That's great news Paul. Congratulations!'

'Yeah, that's terrific news,' said Michael. He leaned over and shook his workmate's hand.

'It would be if I had someplace to stay but.'

'Doesn't your mother live in Tamworth?' asked the old mechanic. 'Why can't you go back to living at home?'

Paul shook his head. 'If I go back ta livin' wiff her, I know I'll end up back inside.'

'It doesn't have to be, if you keep out of trouble.'

'You don't know what it's like at home. Me old lady's always on the grog, and if she ain't been drinkin' she's high as a kite. And once me ol' mates hear I been released, they'll be wantin' me to go out wiff 'em. I just can't go back to livin' that way again.'

'Where else can you stay?' asked Michael.

'There ain't no place else, not unless you let me stay here.'

'What, in the workshop?' The old mechanic was incredulous. 'Are you kidding?'

'Nah, I s'pose not.'

Paul did not say anything further about his impending release or of his accommodation needs. He could not blame George for not wanting him to live in the workshop. If the tables were turned, he would probably not want an ex-convict living in his place of work. He just had to hope that the Prison Welfare Officer could find somewhere suitable for him.

Brian Redmond had been busy, but without success. He had enquired at all the local caravan parks for long-term leasing of an on-site cabin, but the cheapest was $467 per week, which was way more than Paul would be able to afford, even with rental assistance. There were some budget hotels in the area, but with limited cooking facilities, they could hardly be considered suitable. But they were not really a long-term solution anyway. The various real estate agencies in Tamworth had a number of homes and units listed as available for lease, but as soon as he mentioned that he was from Tamworth Correctional Centre, the places were suddenly no longer available.

Brian visited the Aboriginal Housing Office in Tamworth but, with budget constraints, their only advice was for Paul to go back to the family home. They would, however, place his name on a waiting list should a home become available in the future, but the Prison Welfare Officer knew from past experience that there was little chance of that occurring.

When Brian Redmond returned to the prison, he met up with the Parole Officer, Bob Petersen, to give him an update on his search for accommodation for Paul.

'I can't see why he can't return to the family home,' asserted Bob.

'His mother's an alcoholic, and there's been a lot of domestic violence in the home. He's afraid he'll end up back in here,' informed Brian.

'D'ya think that's likely?'

'If his past history's anythin' to go by, yes, I think it's more than likely.'

'Where's he working?'

'At a motorbike workshop just off the New England Highway about five ks south of the city.'

'Have you spoken with them about it yet?'

'What, about his accommodation? I thought I was lucky gettin' Paul a job there. I think asking them to give him a place to stay as well would be stretching the friendship a tad far.'

'Bugger the friendship. Paul's future relies on finding him a place to stay. Do you want me to speak to them?'

'No, I will.'

'Well I'll come too.'

The following morning, after the van had finished delivering all the work-release prisoners to their various places of employment, and had returned to the prison, Brian Redmond, together with Bob Petersen, drove back to the old mechanic's workshop.

When they emerged from the car, they were met by Michael. 'Are you here to check up on Paul?'

'No, actually, we wanna word with you an' George,' informed Brian. 'Mike, this is Bob Petersen. Bob is gonna be Paul's Parole Officer when he's released.'

The two men shook hands.

'Is there a problem?'

'Well yes, as a matter of fact.'

The old mechanic was already busy doing the accounts in Katie's office. He was surprised when he looked up to see the two prison officials enter the room followed by Michael.

'What's up?'

'Hello George, this is Bob Petersen, Paul's Parole Officer. We wanna speak with you an' Mike.'

'Get some chairs Mike,' directed the old mechanic.

When the three men were seated, the old mechanic repeated his question, 'So what's up?"

'Are you aware that the Parole Board has approved Paul's release for next Mond'y?' asked Brian.

'Yeah, he told us yesterd'y,' said the old mechanic.

'It's great news, isn't it?' added Michael enthusiastically.

'It is, but the Board's concerned about the arrangements for his accommodation. They're worried he doesn't have suitable accommodation to go to.'

'What do you mean by "suitable"?' asked the old mechanic.

'"Suitable" is fairly broad in its definition, but basically it's any place where there's not limited tenure, where he's protected from the elements, and where he's safe from abuse or attack.'

'Why can't he go back to livin' with his family?'

'He's not safe in the family home. To escape from the violence at home, he joined a gang. They put pressure on him to commit a string of burglaries, the result being, he ended up back in prison. If he goes back to livin' at home, there's a pretty good chance he'll repeat his past mistakes and end up back inside.'

'There must be some place else that's "suitable",' insisted Michael, 'Tamworth's a big city.'

'It is a big city, but it's also big on prejudice,' informed Bob. 'Every place we've enquired about is either too expensive or no longer available.'

'What about that Aboriginal Housing mob?' suggested the old mechanic, 'I heard they've got lotsa money. They should have somethin' "suitable" for Paul.'

Brian shook his head. 'I enquired at their office too. With budget cuts, they said they don't have anything.'

'So, what're you gonna do?' asked Michael.

Brian turned from Michael to the old mechanic. 'You've been really generous in giving Paul a place to work.'

The old mechanic interrupted the Prison Welfare Officer. 'Before you say anything more, the answer's no!'

'But you don't know what I'm gonna ask.'

'Yes I do. Paul's already asked me if he can stay here in the workshop, and I've already said no. And besides, it's not "suitable" anyway. So, end of story.'

'Actually, I wasn't gonna ask if he could live in the workshop; I agree, I don't think this place is really suitable anyway.'

'So, what were you gonna ask?'

'I understand you live on your own in the cottage across the laneway.'

'You're not gonna suggest he move in with me, are you?'

'As a matter of fact, ...' advised Bob.

'Who d'ya think I am, The Salvation-bloody-Army. The answer's still no.'

There was an embarrassed silence in the room for several moments.

Eventually Michael broke the silence. 'I think it's a great idea.'

'Whose bloody side are you on?' blurted out the old mechanic.

'I'm on no-one's side, and everyone's side. You've been complaining for years about how lonely you are. Here's a solution – Paul's good company. And, your health hasn't been the best of late. If you were to have another heart attack, at night, you might not make it next time. But with Paul around, he'll be able to call the ambulance. It's a win – win.'

'But we haven't even offered him a permanent job yet,' pleaded the old mechanic meekly.

'I don't see why we can't offer him a job now. He's smart, he's eager to learn, he's got a great work ethic, he's conscientious, polite and he's good to work with. He's a good motorcycle mechanic.'

'Oh, I don't know.'

Paul had been working, busily servicing a BSA Golden Flash, while listening to the discussion taking place inside the office. When he had finished the service, he made his way to the doorway and stood quietly, waiting for an opportunity to speak. Slowly, all eyes turned in his direction.

Paul shuffled his feet nervously, unused to the attention, but he was determined to have a say. He cleared his throat and began while avoiding eye contact.

'I c'n understand why you don't want me to stay wiff ya George; you're a white fella and I'm a black fella, we're different as chalk 'n cheese. You don't hafta like me, or like what I done, an' I can't change the past. I can't promise we'll be the best o' mates, and I can't promise we'll agree on everythin'. But I can promise that I'll respect ya and everythin' that belongs to ya. All I ask for is respect in return.'

Bob was about to speak, but Michael cut him off, 'I don't think Paul's finished yet.'

He had not. 'I learned a lot about meself bein' locked up these past few years, and I learned a lot about other people too. I learned about tolerance and gettin' along with people who hated me guts, just because of the colour of me skin. I found I couldn't do anythin' about them, that I could do somethin' about me but an' how *I* responded to *them*.'

Paul's pulse was racing and his mouth was getting dry. He swallowed hard before he continued.

'If ya don' want me ta come an' live with ya, I c'n un'erstand – no hard feelin's. If I was in your place, I might feel the same. But like Mike said, I can look after ya and keep ya company. I know how to cook an' clean, I can help ya wiff the housework an' shoppin' an' stuff, an' I can mow the lawns for ya. An' like he said, it's a win – win. I ain't after charity; I need someplace safe ta stay but. Your place'ld be perfect.'

There was silence for a good few minutes. Eventually, the old mechanic spoke, 'Awright, looks like ya got me by the short an' curlies. Let me think about it, okay?'

Everyone else let out a collective sigh of relief.

'Thanks George.' Brian and Michael spoke together.

'I haven't said yes yet.'

Brian and Bob got to their feet to shake hands with the other two. As they were leaving Brian turned to the old mechanic, 'Can you let me have your answer tomorrow? I need to let the Parole Board know whether or not Paul can be released.'

'Yeah, okay.'

Nothing more was said for the remainder of the day, but there was an air of satisfaction surrounding the two younger mechanics as they conducted their work, servicing a range of classic British motorcycles.

After Paul had departed for the afternoon, Michael approached his father-in-law. 'So, are you gonna say yes?'

'After the speech you and Paul gave, how could I say no?'

'Then why didn't you give them the good news before they left?'

The old mechanic smiled. 'I didn't want them to think I'd caved in too easily.'

'You crafty old bugger.'

Chapter 5

TWO BIRDS WITH THE ONE STONE

Paul did not require an alarm to wake him that following Monday morning; he was awake even before the kookaburra called. Although he had been paroled twice following his previous stints in prison, this time was different, this time he had a job to go to and a new safer place to live. He had already been quizzed about why he was not returning to the family home. Some of the members of his community could not understand his reasoning. But at least Uncle Danny Stewart and some of the other older men understood; after all, they knew his family. He did not care what anyone else thought.

A prison guard had given him his rucksack to pack his belongings, although Paul did not own much. Other than several changes of underwear, a couple of t-shirts, a pair of jeans, a Sloppy Joe, the clothes he wore at Court and a pair of runners, he had few other worldly possessions. The prison had given him a pair of overalls and safety shoes to wear while he was on work-release, which he was allowed to keep. He hoped George would have a bed and spare bedding that he could use. He had very little money to speak of; only the earnings he had received since he had started in the workshop which had gone straight into the bank. He had yet to discuss his boarding costs with the old mechanic, but he hoped they would not be too exorbitant. At least he would not need transport.

Paul thought about the items he had in his room prior to his incarceration – a watch, an alarm clock and an old guitar –

but he knew from past experience that they would probably no longer be at the family home, let alone in his bedroom. One of the things he had come to understand about black fellas compared to the white community was that possessions were communal rather than personal. Belongings were only yours until someone else had a greater need for them. It was this way of thinking that had first brought him into conflict with the law. He knew he would need to modify his outlook when he moved in with the old mechanic.

When the alarm sounded at 6:00 am, Paul was first out of his cell heading to the ablution block to brush his teeth and shave. He had already changed into his civilian clothes, so he stood out from the rest of the prison population. Paul had just lathered up ready to shave when an eerie quiet descended on the room. He looked up into the polished steel mirror to see three prisoners standing around him, all Lebanese. All of the other prisoners had fled.

One of the Lebanese thugs spoke. 'Where d'ya fink you're goin' ya black bastard?'

Paul's heart skipped a beat. In his excitement about leaving the prison he had made the fundamental error of entering the ablution block on his own. Normally, he would wait for other members of his mob, but today he had forgotten.

Now with his pulse racing, Paul tried to turn around, but one of his assailants pinned his arms from behind. He braced for the blow that was sure to come as he was swung around. Even so, when it came the wind was knocked out of him. He would have dropped to the floor had he not been held up. Another of the thugs was about to land a second blow when a group of about a dozen Aboriginal prisoners burst into the room. In an instant, Paul was released, slumping to the floor. The Lebanese thugs went from being the aggressors to suddenly being on the receiving end of a good beating. The guards arrived too late to stop the assault.

The old mechanic and Michael had grown used to Paul arriving late for work, but when he had not turned up by smoko, the older man quizzed his son-in-law, 'Where's Paul?'

Michael shrugged his shoulders. 'I dunno. I guess he's got some business to attend to. He gets released today, so he might be waitin' for a lift.'

'Did he ask anyone?'

'Yeah, I think Uncle Danny Stewart was sortin' somethin' out for him. Why? Are you getting excited about your new house mate?' replied Michael with a grin.

'Yeah, sure!'

'Oh, I just remembered, he's booked in for a riding test to get his bike licence this morning, so we might not see him 'til after lunch.'

'Where's he gettin' the bike from to do the test?'

'The Riding School supplies a Honda CB250. I think Correctional Services pays for it as part of Paul's rehab.'

'Correctional Services? You mean our taxes.'

'Yeah, something like that. But if it means people like Paul don't reoffend, I reckon it's a good investment.'

'Yeah, I s'pose.'

The old mechanic's health and fitness had been gradually improving, such that he had recently traded the walking frame for a walking stick. He was still much weaker, and thus slower, than he had been prior to his heart attack, but he was now able to complete a wider range of maintenance tasks on their customers' bikes. However, the effort to kick-start an engine was just too great for him, so he was still unable to take a motorcycle for a test ride, leaving that task to Michael.

Uncle Danny Stewart had initially planned to have one of Paul's cousins pick him up from the prison gates at 8:00 am and take him to his home, but Paul was none too happy with that arrangement. He did not want to be left at the family home for *any* amount of time, especially as his mother was likely still drinking. So, the parolee had to bide his time sitting under the awning outside the security office until the Elder was free so that he could take him to the licence testing facility and thence to the old mechanic's workshop. It was mid morning before the old Holden Commodore station wagon made its way into the prison carpark.

Paul greeted his mentor. 'Hi Uncle Danny, thanks for pickin' me up.'

'Hi Paulie.'

Paul threw his rucksack into the backseat and hopped into the front. He winced with pain at the effort, holding his left side.

'What's up?' asked Uncle Danny.

'Oh nothin', I just got punched by one of the Lebs.'

'You awright?'

Paul smiled. 'Yeah, I'm a lot better 'an he is.'

'Did ya take a deep breath?'

'No, why?'

'Doesn't free air taste so much better than prison air?'

The young man smiled again and breathed deeply. 'It certainly tastes fresher.'

'D'ya wanna go see ya mama? She wants ta see you.'

'I've got a licence test at 11:00, so I need to do that first.'

The journey from the Tamworth Correctional Centre to Wheel Skills, the company that carries out the MOST (Motorcycle Operator Skills Test) on behalf of the NSW Roads and Maritime Services, only takes about 10 minutes. When they were clear of the prison carpark, Uncle Danny asked, 'Are ya nervous?'

'Nah, not really. I'm more excited than anythin'.'

'What're ya excited about?'

'I've been set free. I got a new job and someplace new ta live. It's like I bin born ag'in.'

The Kamilaroi Elder looked across at the younger man as he remembered without rancour his time as a young boy on the Aboriginal mission where he was told that he needed to be "born again". Like so many of his generation, he had been taken from his mother as a child and brought up to learn the white man's ways. He too had spent time in prison, an angry young man, stuck between two cultures. He did not learn about his own culture until he was a man of about Paul's age. He had the older men of his mob to thank for saving him. Now, he was giving back.

'Jus' make sure ya make the most of bein' born ag'in Paulie. Ya might not git another chance.'

'I will, Uncle Danny, I will.'

Paul breezed through the MOST without the loss of any points. With his newly issued P1 Provisional Motorcycle Licence, for the first time in his life he was able to legally ride a motorcycle on the street in the state, albeit one that was LAMS approved. He was beaming when he climbed back into the front seat of the station wagon, although his side continued to trouble him.

'D'ya wanna go see ya mama now?' asked Uncle Danny.

'I'd rather get somethin' ta eat first; I'm starvin'.'

The Kamilaroi Elder turned to face his young charge. 'Don' cha wanna go see 'er?'

'I don't wanna get into a fight about why I ain't comin' home ta live. She won't understand, even if she hasn't been drinkin'.'

Uncle Danny could not argue with Paul. The last time he had seen Lynette Tracey, she had been sitting on a urine-soaked lounge chair, a flagon of cheap Muscat in one hand and a cigarette in the other, screaming profanities to anyone within earshot. He shuddered at the thought.

'Wha' d'ya wanna eat?'

'I haven't had a Maccas for more 'an three years. I've been dreamin' of a Big Mac for the past six moths.'

The Kamilaroi Elder smiled. 'You should have bigger dreams.'

The old mechanic and Michael were just finishing lunch when the old Holden station wagon pulled up in the laneway outside the workshop. The two men rose to meet the car.

When the Aboriginal mechanic opened his door, Michael asked, 'How'd ya go?'

Paul responded by holding up his new Provisional Licence.

'Yoo-hoo, well done.'

Paul flashed a smile. 'I'm legal now, and free at last.'

The old mechanic joined the others. 'How does it feel?'

'As I said to Uncle Danny, it's like I bin born ag'in.'

'Have you had lunch yet?' asked Michael.

'Yeah, we dropped in at McDonalds on the way here.'

The old mechanic screwed up his nose. 'Your first meal as a free man, and you had to choose Maccas.'

Paul laughed. 'I might 'ave bin a free man, but the meal was anythin' but. I don't fink I'll be able to afford to go back there any time soon.'

'Yeah, well livin' with me you certainly won't be gettin' burgers very often.'

Paul retrieved his rucksack from the back of the station wagon, allowing Uncle Danny to leave.

'Come! I'll show you where you're gonna sleep.'

Paul obediently followed the old mechanic across the backyard of the cottage, up the ramp and through the small kitchen to the bedroom that was once Katie's. The pop idol posters on the walls had been removed, the dolls put away and the girly furnishings replaced with more neutral items; the room was now more suited to the new occupant.

'Who us'ta sleep here?'

'Katie.'

'I hope she don't mind me usin' her room.'

'With any luck, she won't be needin' it again. The bathroom's at the end of the hall and the toilet's next to that. The laundry's next to the kitchen. There's a spare towel in the linen press. If you need anythin', just ask.'

'Where's your room?'

'Across the hall.'

The old mechanic gave his new boarder a key to the house and left him to change into his work clothes. Paul sat on the bed; it was softer than anything he had ever slept on, and certainly much more comfortable than the hard vinyl covered mattress on the concrete pad he had grown used to in his prison cell. If anything, his new bed was too comfortable, but he was sure that, in time, he would get used to it. Besides, he thought, he could always sleep on the floor. He quickly changed and left the house, massaging his side. He locked the door behind him, a task that, until that morning, was the guard's responsibility.

Under Michael's direction, Paul began his first task as a free man with renewed enthusiasm, servicing a BSA 500cc Shooting Star. As he worked, he thought about how his circumstances had changed for the better since he had completed his Motorcycle Mechanics Apprentice Course.

Up until he had come to work for Michael, he had only ever had bad experiences with the white community; the cops, the magistrates, his lawyers, and the prison guards and staff were all white fellas. But since he had started in the workshop, he began to see them from a different perspective. He was glad that he had met Michael and George, and grateful for what they were now doing for him.

Before long, it was time for their afternoon break.

While the three men waited for the jug to boil, Michael asked, 'If you're on parole, do you need to report to the local cop shop or anythin' like that?'

'Nah, the Parole Officer, you know, Bob Petersen, the guy who was here last week with Brian, he comes around visitin' workplaces or where ya livin' to see how ya doin'.'

'So, he's like a Welfare Officer for parolees,' said the old mechanic.

'Yeah, somethin' like that.'

'At least with you livin' and workin' at the same place, he can kill two birds with the one stone.'

Chapter 6

GOOD THINGS

The left side of Paul's abdomen, where he had been punched, was still tender. But not wishing to make a fuss, he said nothing to either Michael or the old mechanic. He had grown used to the prison van arriving around 4:00 pm, signalling that it was time to leave, but it did not arrive that afternoon, so Paul kept working.

'You might be livin' here now, but that doesn't mean ya hafta work extra hours,' called the old mechanic. 'It's past your knock-off time.'

'What time is it?'

'Twenty to five.'

'Sorry,' conceded Michael, 'I should've said somethin' earlier. I just didn't think about it.'

'That's awright Mike,' replied Paul, 'I don't mind workin' late 'cos I didn't start 'til after lunch. Besides, it's not as if I've got a missus to go home to.'

'Yeah, but we've still got dinner to prepare,' said the old mechanic.

'What're we havin'?'

'Steak, chips 'n salad.'

'Hmm, that's better than I would've got in prison.'

'And better than you'd get at McDonalds too, I'll wager.'

'You don't like Maccas, do you?' said Michael.

'Their coffee's alright. It's their burgers I don't like. Their buns are too sweet and their cheese's disgusting.'

'I'll remember that.'

'We're off then, Mike. We'll see ya tomorrow.'

'Okay, see ya. Enjoy the steak Paul.'

'I will.'

Paul followed the old mechanic across the lane and up the ramp to the back door of the small cottage, while Michael locked up the workshop and left on his Norton.

'I only need ta wash me hands,' advised the old mechanic, 'so you c'n have first use of the shower, if you like. I'll make a start on dinner.'

Paul found a clean towel in the linen press and made his way to the bathroom. He smiled at his reflection in the mirror. Over the past three and a half years he had only ever seen a hazy image of himself, because the prison did not allow glass mirrors. As he stood naked in the shower, he felt the left side of his abdomen again. If anything, it was even more painful now than it had been when he was first punched.

All scrubbed clean and now wearing his jeans and a t-shirt, he returned to the kitchen to see if the old mechanic needed a hand. But the pained look on his face betrayed how he was feeling.

'Are you awright?'

'Yeah, I jus' got a pain in me guts.'

'Have you got a touch of gastro? See, I told you those burgers were no good.'

'Nah, it wasn't the burger. One of the Lebs punched me this morning while I was shavin'. I think it was me goin' away present. I thought it'd be okay; it's real sore now but.'

'I think you need to see a doctor.'

Paul did not argue.

After replacing the food back into the refrigerator, the old mechanic opened up the workshop and drove out his old Ford Ranger utility. The effort was taxing his fitness, but at the moment, Paul's needs were greater than his own. He drove his young boarder to the Accident and Emergency Department of Tamworth Base Hospital. Being a Monday night, it was relatively quiet. After a short wait, Paul was examined by an intern, who sent him for a CT scan. The scan revealed a small tear in his spleen so he was admitted overnight for observation.

The old mechanic arrived early the following morning, although Michael still beat him and was already dealing with their customers when he walked in. He went straight to the jug and filled it for the morning's first cuppa. Eventually, his son-in-law joined him.

'Where's Paul?'
'In hospital.'
'What happened?' Michael was alarmed.
'He didn't give me all the details, but it appears one of the other prisoners assaulted him before he left yesterday morning.'
'Is he alright?'
'Yeah, the doctor said he's got a small tear in his spleen.'
'When's he gettin' released?'
'You mean discharged. You're released from prison, but you're discharged from a hospital.'
'Yeah, whatever.'
'Maybe today, maybe tomorrow. It just depends on how he recovers.'
'A ruptured spleen's pretty serious,' Michael declared.
'Yeah, I once knew a bloke who died after his spleen was ruptured in a car crash.'
'Gee, does Paul know who did it? He should tell the cops.'
'I don't think Paul wants to go anywhere near the police at the present time.'
'Yeah, I s'pose.'

'But he should probably let his Parole Officer know.'

'Do you think we should call him?'

'No! Leave it to Paul.' The old mechanic was eager to change the subject so he asked, 'So, what's on the agenda for today?'

'Bikes, bikes, and more bikes. The same as yesterday, and the same as tomorrow.'

'You sound like you're gettin' tired of fixin' these old machines. Is there a problem you're not tellin' me about?'

'No, not really. But I am tired. The baby's still not sleepin' through, an' Katie's tired and grumpy, so she's gettin' crabby with me, and …'

The old mechanic laughed. 'Welcome to fatherhood Mike. In years to come you'll look back and wonder what all the fuss's about. Just be thankful you only have one.'

'Yeah well that's another thing. Katie wants to try for one more, only she wants a girl next time.'

The old mechanic laughed again. 'Do you want my advice Mike?'

'Yeah.'

'Go for it.'

Michael was about to speak further, but his train of thought was interrupted by a vehicle being driven up the laneway outside. The vehicle was a white Toyota Hilux 4WD and it was being driven by John Traeghier, father of Kieran. Both the old mechanic and Michael rose to meet John as he emerged from the vehicle's cabin.

'G'day John, good to see you.' The old mechanic welcomed the visitor.

'Hi John,' echoed Michael.

'Morning George, Mike.' The men all shook hands.

'How's business?' The old mechanic tried to keep the mood light.

'Yeah, it's okay. Fact is, it's prob'ly the only thin' keepin' me sane at the moment.'

'D'ya wanna cuppa. We've just had one, but we could always do with another.'

'Yeah, awright.'

'Tea or coffee?' asked Michael.

'Whatever you have.'

While Michael made everyone a cuppa, the old mechanic sat down with John.

'I heard you ain't been too crash hot lately.' John directed his comment at the old mechanic.

'Yeah, bad news travels fast, but I'm on the mend now. All those years smokin' have finally caught up with me.'

'Yeah, ya never know when ya number's gonna be up. We spend years abusin' our bodies and live inta old age, an' then someone like Kieran comes along, 'is 'ole life still ahead of 'im, an' 'e gets taken in 'is prime.'

'It doesn't seem fair, does it?' added Michael.

'Nah, that's for bloody sure.'

'We've still got his bike over there under that tarp.' The old mechanic pointed to the Triumph Bonneville in the back of the workshop. 'Are you here to take it home?'

'Nah, I don' ever wanna see it again. I'm sorry I ever encouraged Kieran ta restore it.'

'Wha' dya want me to do with it then?'

'I don' give a stuff. Fix it up 'n sell it, break it up for spares, take it to the dump, I don't give a rat's arse.'

John handed the registration papers over to the old mechanic.

'If I fix it up and sell it, I'll send you what I make from it.'

'George, I don't wan' it. Give it to a charity for all I care. It's blood money as far as I'm concerned.'

'Okay.'

Michael took leave of the other two, as he needed to make a start on the customer bikes in the workshop. The old mechanic and John talked for over an hour. It was clear to the old mechanic that John needed time away from the twin stressors of his life: home and work. He was still evidently grieving, trying to cope with the loss of his only son who was also his best friend. At least he was gratified that Kieran's name would live on in the person of Katie and Michael's new baby.

Paul had never spent time in a hospital before. While he had suffered the usual cuts and scrapes as a youth treading on broken glass or falling off a pushbike, he had only ever been treated in a doctor's surgery or a medical clinic. So, it was a real treat for him to be in a hospital ward where he was served his meals in bed. But like so many good things, it was soon cut short when, after two days, the hospital registrar told him he could go home. The old mechanic and Michael had just stopped for their morning smoko when the telephone rang.

'Hello, Classic Bike Repairs and Service, Mike speaking.'
'*Hello Mike, it's Paul.*'
'Hey Paul, how're you feelin'?'
'*They're lettin' me out, can you come 'n pick me up?*'
'Umm, okay. I'm pretty busy right now, but someone'll come an' get you. Where'll you be?'
'*At the hospital. I'll be out front where the ambulance comes in.*'
'Okay, we'll be there in about half an hour.'
'*Okay, see ya.*'
'Yeah bye.'

Paul was quiet on the short trip home, so the old mechanic encouraged him to talk.
'Did they treat you well in the hospital?'
'Yeah, pretty good.'

'How was the food?'

'Yeah, awright. Better 'an the stuff we used ta get in gaol.'

'That's hardly a ringing endorsement.'

Paul flashed a wide smile. 'The nurses were pretty, but.'

It was now the old mechanic's turn to smile. 'Have you had a girlfriend before?'

Now immediately serious, Paul replied with a curt, 'Nah!'

'Not even at school?'

'Nah!'

'Do you have any sisters?'

'Yeah, they don't live 'round here no more but. They all left 'ome when I was little. I ain't seen 'em in a few years.'

'Don't they ever visit ya mum?'

Paul hesitated before replying in a low voice. 'Nobody ever visits mum, 'cept maybe the cops or Welfare.'

'I thought family was important in Aboriginal communities.'

Paul did not reply. The old mechanic realised too late that this was not a topic that the young Aboriginal was comfortable discussing. Mercifully, they soon arrived back at the workshop. While the old mechanic parked the truck, Paul dashed into the house to change into his work clothes.

The three mechanics were very busy, servicing and repairing a variety of classic British motorcycles: BSAs, Nortons and Triumphs mostly. But there was also a rare Matchless G15 CSR 750cc factory café racer that was in for a service. At 11:15, Michael made the short journey to the sandwich shop. His return signalled it was time for lunch.

As the men sat around munching on their sandwiches, Michael asked, 'Have you ever seen one of those Matchies before?'

'Yeah, but not for a while. It's what they call a hybrid. D'ya remember when we had that Norton N15 some time back?'

'Yeah, I think so.'

'Well, the Matchless G15 is its twin. It uses a Norton Atlas 750cc motor, Norton forks and rims, an AMC gearbox and a Matchless frame.'

'Hybrid? It sounds like a bitza,' remarked Paul, 'bitza this an' bitza that.'

The old mechanic laughed. 'It was the original parts-bin special. Speaking of specials, have you ever owned a motorcycle Paul?'

'What, one you could ride on the road without gettin' busted by the cops?'

'Yeah, that sort.'

'Nah.' He shook his head as he spoke.

'How would you like a Triumph Bonneville.'

'What, to keep?'

'Yeah. It needs work, and you'd need to bring it back to standard spec so that you can legally ride it on your Ps.'

'Where is it?'

'Over there under that tarp.' The old mechanic pointed to the machine at the back of the workshop.

'But that's Kieran's bike,' protested Michael.

'Not any more it's not. You heard John. It's mine now and I c'n do with it as I please. So, it pleases me to give it to Paul.'

Michael did not reply. The two younger mechanics were quiet as they finished their lunches, each lost in his own thoughts.

Once the sandwiches were finished, Michael abruptly stood. 'C'mon Paul, we've gotta mountain o' work to get through.'

Paul remained seated. Suddenly a tear began to course down his right cheek. He sniffed before speaking in a low voice that only the old mechanic could hear, 'Good things aren't s'posed to happen to me.'

The old mechanic replied in a similarly low voice. 'Hopefully Paul, this is just the start of many more good things happenin' to you.'

Chapter 7

THE UGLY FACE

The three men broke for their mid-afternoon smoko. Michael was unusually quiet as he made his tea. The old mechanic could see that there was something bothering his son-in-law, but he waited until they had finished their drinks before saying anything.

'Mike, can I have a word?'

Michael followed his father-in-law into the office. The old mechanic closed the door.

'What's up?' asked Michael innocently.

'I was gonna ask you the same question.'

'Nothin's the matter with me.'

'Yeah, pull the other one Mike, it plays Jingle Bells. Somethin's buggin' you, and I wanna know what it is.'

'Nothin's buggin' me,' said Michael.

'Are you upset because I gave Kieran's bike to Paul?'

Michael did not answer at once, but lowered his head as his face turned a shade of red. Eventually, he replied, 'You should've asked me first.'

'What, about givin' the bike to Paul?'

'No, you should've asked me first if I wanted the bike.'

'But you've already got a bike.'

'Yeah, but Kieran's bike's special. It's got all those trick bits o' kit on it.'

'Mike, your bike is every bit as trick. And it has that special ingredient that no other machine has.'

'What's that?'

'It was restored by you, so it's got a piece of you in it; your DNA is all over it. Countless hours and all your blood, sweat and tears have gone into that Norton. And besides, you already told me you couldn't bear to get rid of it, and I'm pretty sure you can't afford two machines. Can you?'

'Umm, no.'

'Givin' it to Paul's the best option. Just as your bike has a little bit of you in it, so Kieran's bike has a little bit of him. Givin' it to Paul is like keepin' a bit of Kieran with us here.'

'Yeah, but what if he leaves?'

'I can't see that happenin' any time soon. And besides, where's he gonna go?'

The rhetorical question remained unanswered. Eventually Michael apologised. 'I'm sorry.'

'That's alright, but Mike, if somethin' I've done upsets you, don't stew on it. Come an' talk ta me.'

'Yeah, I will.'

The two men embraced before Michael returned to the workshop to continue servicing a customer's AJS.

'Is everythin' awright?' asked Paul from behind the Triumph Trident he was working on.

'Yeah, everythin's fine.'

'Were you cranky with George about him givin' me Kieran's bike?'

'Nah, I'm okay about it. I suppose I still miss him a lot.'

'Were you good mates?'

'Yeah, we were great mates.'

'Was he a good bike mechanic too?'

'Kieran? Kieran was the best ... better than I'll ever be.'

Hopefully, I'm gonna be the best too one day, thought Paul to himself.

Later that evening over dinner Paul asked the old mechanic, 'Wha' didja mean when ya said I had to bring the Bonneville back to standard spec? What spec is it in now?'

'When Kieran restored it, he fitted 750cc barrels and pistons to it, bigger valves and a lumpier cam. While you're on your Ps, the largest capacity bike you can legally ride is 660cc.'

'Can anyone tell from the outside if the bike's got a bigger motor?'

'Umm, no, probably not.'

'So who's gonna stop me from ridin' it if no-one c'n tell.'

'I am. While ever you're workin' and livin' here, you'll be ridin' within the law, or not at all.'

Suitably chastened, Paul was silent for a few minutes as he ate some more of his meal. Eventually he tried another tack. 'But what're we gonna do with the larger barrels an' stuff? It'd be a waste if we don't use 'em.'

'They've hardly done any miles, so we c'n put 'em aside. Then when you're off your Provisional Licence, you can fit them back on, if that's what you want.'

'Where're we gonna get the standard parts from?'

'We'll have to shop around. eBay's a good place to start.'

'I've never used eBay before.'

'Well, now's a good time to begin.'

When the table was cleared and the dirty dishes washed and put away, the old mechanic turned on the laptop computer to begin a search for the parts needed to restore the 1963 Triumph Bonneville to its former glory. The required parts were relatively easy to find given the popularity of the model. By the time the two men were ready for bed, they had placed bids on everything they needed.

After the interruption caused by his hospitalisation, Paul had yet to sleep in his new bed, so he was excited about going to bed that night. He still felt strange sleeping in Katie's old room, especially as there was still a faint smell of her perfume in the pillow. Paul did not own any pyjamas so he slept in his undies. He had thought of sleeping nude, as he used to at home, but decided against it, just in case he should get up during the night and in doing so offend his host. The night was cool, the bed warm and he was tired so he drifted off fairly quickly.

Paul awoke in the early hours of the morning. The dawn had yet to make an appearance on the eastern horizon. He was momentarily disoriented, unsure of where he was, but then he remembered. He snuggled down under the covers and tried to go back to sleep, but he was already awake now. The house was eerily quiet, so unlike the prison, the hospital or his family home. Somewhere in the distance a rooster was crowing, rather than a kookaburra, signalling that the sunrise would soon be on its way.

After flinging the bedclothes aside Paul fumbled with the light-switch on the bedside lamp. He shielded his eyes while they adjusted to the glare of the bare globe. He did not know what time it was but guessed it was sometime before 6:00 am. He dressed quickly and, after a brief visit to the toilet, made his way into the kitchen.

The old mechanic had left the toaster out with instructions on where to find bread and a variety of toppings. He had also left the coffee and sugar, as well as mugs, on the kitchen bench. Paul tried to move around quietly for fear of waking his host, but he need not have bothered as the old mechanic was already awake. Still dressed in his pyjamas, he was yawning when he entered the kitchen.

'Mornin' George.'
'Hi Paul, how'd ya sleep?'
'Like a log. Wha' about you?'

'Yeah, alright. How was the bed, was it comf'table enough?'

Paul laughed. 'It was nearly too comf'table.'

'Why'd ya get up so early? The workshop doesn't hafta open 'til seven.'

Paul shrugged his shoulders. 'I dunno, I had enough sleep I s'pose.'

'Well, just remember: this's home and over there's work, and never the twain shall meet.'

'Wha' d'ya mean?'

'What I mean is, there's a separation. Just because you live next to the workshop, doesn't mean you have to be in work mode all the time.'

'Yeah, but I love me work, an' I love workin' here. I don't mind doin' extra hours.'

'Well, just you mark my words.'

'Okay, I will.'

Paul filled the jug and inserted a couple of slices of frozen bread into the toaster. He found the peanut butter in the cupboard and the strawberry jam in the refrigerator. While the bread was toasting, he spooned the coffee and sugar into one of the mugs.

'Why d'ya put the bread in the freezer?' asked Paul.

'It doesn't get stale that way.'

'It doesn't get stale if ya jus' eadit faster.'

'Yeah, well now that we've got two people eatin' it, we might jus' be able to make the change.'

'We both prob'ly need ta make some changes.'

Paul could not wait to begin his first full day of work as a free man. He met Michael as he climbed off his bike and helped to open up the workshop. While Michael dealt with a number of their customers, Paul made a start servicing a BSA 650cc Lightning.

'Hey Paul, come an' have a cuppa coffee,' the old mechanic called after he had filled and turned on the jug.'

'I already had one at breakfast.'

'Well, come an' sit down for a bit.'

Paul reluctantly left the classic Beeza and joined Michael and the old mechanic who had both just started drinking their mugs of tea.

'What's up?' asked Paul.

'Nothing's up,' replied Michael, 'this is just how we always start the day. We talk about what we're each gonna be doin' over a cuppa.'

'But I awready know what I'm gonna be doin'.'

'And what's that?'

'Fixin' bikes.'

The old mechanic took up the argument. 'Paul, this is the time we come together to discuss issues, resolve problems and to impart knowledge. It's where we learn from one another. Our work isn't just fixin' these classic motorbikes. Those who ride them aren't just the owners, they're actually the temporary custodians of these wonderful old machines. So, our job is to act as stewards to ensure they remain in the best possible runnin' condition.'

'Umm, I never knew that.'

After their first break of the day, Paul resumed his work on the Lightning while Michael began replacing the front brake pads on a Norton Commando Mk 2A Interstate. Meanwhile, the old mechanic took up his role sorting through the finances of the business, a job he endured rather than enjoyed.

When the three men broke again for smoko, the old mechanic asked, 'So when's Katie comin' back to work?'

'I think she's still got about a month to go. Why, are ya gettin' sick of doin' her job?'

'You better believe it.'

'Hey Mike, can I go an' get the lunches today. Seein' I ain't a prisoner no more, I don't hafta stay in the workshop all the time.'

'Yeah, I don't see why not. I'll give you some money before you go. But we've still got some work to get through before lunchtime.'

Paul was excited at the prospect of going shopping, even if it was only for sandwiches. At 11:45, Michael gave him enough money for the lunches for the three mechanics. After getting directions to the shop, Paul took off like an eager schoolboy.

The sandwich shop they usually bought their lunches from was about half a kilometre from the workshop. Paul arrived in around five minutes. The doorbell chimed as he entered. There were no other customers inside, and just one young woman serving.

Paul was just about to place his order when a voice from the doorway behind the counter called out. 'What do you want?' The gruff voice belonged to a middle-aged balding man with wisps of grey hair above his ears. The young shop assistant escaped through the door.

'I wanna order some samyges.' Paul had met people like the bald man before, so he stood his ground.

'We don't serve your type 'round here, now piss orf.'

'But I work for …' Paul did not get a chance to finish what he had to stay.

'I don't give a damn who you work for, now get outta my shop before I throw you out.' The bald man came out from behind the counter and approached Paul in an aggressive manner.

Paul was angry, but where once he would have retaliated and sent objects crashing to the floor, he left and made his way quickly back to the workshop. On the surface he was calm, but inwardly, he was seething.

Michael met him as he arrived. 'Where're the lunches? Did you lose the money I gave you?'

'The racist bastards wouldn't serve me?' Paul was almost in tears.

The old mechanic emerged from the office. 'What?'

'They told me to piss orf; they didn't serve my type there.'

'Where'd you go?'

'The shop Mike told me to.'

'And they wouldn't serve you?'

'They told me to piss orf.'

'Who told you?'

'The old man with the bald head.'

Mike was outraged. 'I'll go down there 'n sort it out.'

'No Mike,' replied the old mechanic, 'I'll go. Paul, come with me.'

The old mechanic jumped into the Ford Ranger utility with Paul in the passenger seat. He drove the short distance to the sandwich shop and pulled up out the front. Both men got out of the vehicle.

'Wait outside a minute.'

The old mechanic pushed open the shop door. The doorbell chimed as he entered.

The shop assistant called to him as he approached the counter. 'Hello Mr Edwards, how are you today?'

'I'm fine thanks Jessie. Is your boss in?'

Before Jessie could call him, the bald man entered the shop from the back room. 'Hello George, long time no see. How can I help you?'

'How long have I been coming to this shop Graeme?'

'Oh, I dunno, a long time. Since I was a young boy in short pants. Why?'

'And in all that time, how loyal have I been to you and your family?'

Graeme was beginning to feel uncomfortable. 'Umm, you've been very loyal. I can't remember a week when you haven't got your lunches from here. Why, is there a problem?'

'Yes, there is a problem. Why'd you tell my new mechanic to piss off, and that you didn't serve his type here. What type do you serve here?'

Graeme's face started to turn red. 'Umm, err …'

The old mechanic turned back to the door. 'Paul, come in here.' Paul re-entered the shop. 'Is this the man who told you to piss off, and that they didn't serve your type here?'

'Yes.'

'You haven't heard the last of this Graeme.'

The sandwich shop owner started to panic. 'But he … I, umm, I didn't know he worked for you George. He didn't tell me.'

'You didn't give me a chance,' said Paul.

'What does it matter who he works for?'

Chapter 8

PAYING THE PRICE

When he returned to the workshop, the old mechanic was still angry about the treatment Paul received at the hands of the sandwich shop owner, even if the Aboriginal mechanic now seemed relatively unconcerned. While he had seen racist behaviour on television, he had never witnessed it at close hand. He had thought of taking his business elsewhere, but decided to give Graeme the chance to redeem himself, especially when the next nearest sandwich shop was another two kilometres further in to town. He and Paul accepted the owner's grovelling apology, as well as the offer of free sandwiches for their lunch.

As the three men sat down with their sandwiches, the old mechanic asked, 'Do you come up against racism very often?'

Paul laughed. 'Everywhere, all the time.'

'How do you put up with it?' Michael was appalled.

'You jus' get used to it. Sometimes if ya do somethin' about it the cops get involved and, some of them are jus' as bad, if not worse. An' when you're an ex-con, if anythin' bad happens, the cops'll be 'round to lock ya up, even if ya ain't done nothin'.'

The old mechanic smiled at the double negative, but said nothing. He understood exactly what Paul meant.

'There are two laws in this country, one for the white man, and one for the black fella.'

'I always thought that too,' affirmed Michael, 'but I always thought it was in favour of the blacks.'

'Ha! Why d'ya think there're so many black fellas locked up in gaol but? It ain't 'cos we're worse 'an anyone else.'

'There are criminals in all communities.' The old mechanic made an attempt to placate Paul.

'Yeah, but why're there more of us in gaol?'

The question lingered in the air like a bad smell that would not go away. Australia was supposed to be a tolerant, pluralistic, multiracial, multicultural society. We do not like to think of ourselves as racist or intolerant.

At last Michael jumped to his feet. 'We haven't got time to fix all the problems of the world right now; we've got work to do.'

The old mechanic breathed a sigh of relief. Thanks Mike, he said to himself.

While Michael started sorting out the electrical gremlins on a Norton Atlas and the old mechanic placed an order for spare parts, Paul set about servicing a tired Ariel Huntmaster 650cc twin. The motor had been running roughly, the tappets rattled noisily at idle and there was the telltale puff of bluish smoke when the throttle was shut off, suggesting a sticking valve. The motor really needed a top-end refresh, but the owner was tight with his money and only wanted the absolute minimum carried out: the carburettor float bowl cleaned, the timing adjusted and the contact breaker points cleaned and adjusted.

Paul was having difficulty adjusting the timing on the old machine. There seemed to be a fair amount of play in the bearing and just when he thought he had it right, the backing plate would move and the timing would be out again. He worked on it for over an hour, swearing and cursing under his breath as he laboured, but he did not ask for assistance, so the others kept their distance. Eventually he moved on and started working on the carburettor.

'Did ya manage to get the timin' right on the Ariel Paul?' asked the old mechanic over their afternoon smoko.

'It's nearly right. There's a lot of slop in the bearin', but it's close enough.'

'If it's nearly right, that means it's wrong. Close enough is never good enough.'

'But the backin' plate keeps movin'. I don't reckon anyone could get it a hundred percent right.'

'If that's the case, and I don't doubt you, then we should let the owner know. He can then decide on a course of action. If we can't repair a machine to the maker's specs, then we need to tell the owner, not keep quiet about it and hope he doesn't notice.'

'But what about all the time I already spent tryin' to gedit right? He still needs to pay for it.'

'Not if you haven't fixed his bike.'

Michael broke into the conversation. 'There are swings and roundabouts Paul. We can always make it up on another machine.'

'But that's not fair. The owner of this ol' heap o' junk gets away without payin' for all the time I put in tryin' to fix it.'

The old mechanic laughed. 'Life's not fair Paul. As the sayin' goes, "Life's a bitch, an' then ya die." If life was fair, no-one would cheat, lie or steal; everyone would do the right thing by everyone else. And we wouldn't need police, lawyers, magistrates or gaols.'

'And no-one would hurt anyone else, either physically or verbally,' added Michael.

There was a pause while everyone thought again about the sandwich shop owner's verbal assault on the young Aboriginal earlier in the day.

Eventually Paul informed the others, 'I could do without cops, lawyers, magistrates and gaols but.'

Everyone laughed.

When the old mechanic returned from a brief visit to the bathroom, he found Michael and Paul in a vigorous debate about politics. With the approaching election, they were discussing the pros and cons of both sides – the free-market conservatives of the Coalition and the socialist-leaning Labor. He rarely shared his opinions about which side was better in government, so he did not say anything until Michael looked to him for support.

'I think there's good and bad on both sides. You know, my old man once said to me, "Son," he said, "the difference between Capitalism and Socialism is that in Capitalism, man exploits man."'

'See,' jumped in Paul, 'I told ya.'

The old mechanic held up his hand to signify that he had not finished. '"And in Socialism, it's the other way around."'

Michael laughed. Paul did not comprehend at first, but smiled when it eventually occurred to him what was said.

The old mechanic continued. 'The problem isn't about which side is better or worse than the other, right or left, capitalism or socialism, the Coalition or Labor. The problem isn't the system, exploitation occurs on both sides. The problem is greed. Some years ago, there was a movie where one of the characters declared: "Greed is good." Well, I don't think anything could be further from the truth. Greed fuels exploitation. Greedy banks exploit their customers by chargin' exorbitant fees, and greedy corporations exploit their workers by underpayin' them. But greedy union leaders exploit their members by misusin' union funds. Even politicians have been known to exploit the votin' public by the misuse of electoral funds.'

'But who should we vote for then?' asked Paul.

'I'm not gonna say who *you* should vote for. But *I* would vote for the party that *I* reckon would create an environment where exploitation is minimised.'

'But if greed's the problem,' posed Michael, 'wouldn't it be better to vote for the party that is less likely to foster an environment for greed?'

'And which party would that be Mike?' asked the old mechanic.

Michael thought for a moment before shrugging his shoulders. 'I dunno.'

Paul was silent.

'You can't legislate for greed, but you can legislate for exploitation. If greed is like a disease, exploitation is the symptom that results. In a perfect world, we could treat the disease. But we can't, so we just have to treat the symptom – legislation is the treatment.'

'Speakin' of exploitation, if we don't get these bikes finished, we're not gonna make any money this arvo, so my bank manager might have to start exploitin' me.'

The other two laughed.

It was nearly 5:00 pm before all three mechanics had finished their respective tasks, even with the old mechanic helping to service an AJS Model 33 belonging to one of their customers. While Michael closed and locked the workshop, the other two headed for home. Now almost routine, Paul headed straight for the shower while the old mechanic began preparing dinner – bangers and mash.

With the sausages sizzling in a frypan and the potatoes bubbling away in a saucepan, the old mechanic placed a couple of servings of mixed vegetables in the microwave. Paul joined him and started setting the table.

'Are we havin' gravy or do you want tomato sauce?'

'I'll have dead 'orse.'

Paul smiled. 'That's what some of the old fellas in gaol called it.'

'What, dead 'orse? Yeah, you don't hear rhymin' slang much nowadays. I think we listen to too much American slang on the tele. Good ol' Aussie slang nearly gets forgotten.'

'Why do people use slang?'

The old mechanic thought for a moment. 'Language is all about communication. Sometimes usin' slang is the best way of gettin' the message over. Same as some people who swear a lot. I know some blokes, every second word's a swear word. But for them, that's how they speak; it's how they communicate.'

'You don't swear very much.'

'Yeah, I never learned to. My dad was a strict churchman. He reckoned swearin' reflected a weakness of character. He never allowed me to swear growin' up or in the workshop. And after I got married, I didn't wanna swear in front of me missus or Katie. When you get into the habit of doing somethin' for so long, you just keep doin' it, or in my case, not doin' it.'

The two men sat down to their meal. As they ate, they talked about a whole range of topics: motorbikes, growing up, school and friends. The old mechanic prudently avoided raising the subject of family again, and in particular Paul's.

As they finished their meal, Paul said, 'No white fella's ever stuck up for me before.'

'What, you mean like I did at the sandwich shop?'

'Yeah.'

'Not even at school or in the gaol?'

'Nah.'

'That prison social worker did.'

'Yeah, that was his job but.'

'Well, it was my job to stick up for you today.'

'Yeah, but ya didn't hafta. You coulda jus' asked Mike to go an' get the lunches.'

'But that wouldn't have been fair on you, or on Mike.'

'But standin' up for me coulda meant you would've had to go to another shop, after ya been goin' there for all them years.'

'Yeah, well that was the price I was prepared ta pay.'

'Ya didn't hafta but.'

The old mechanic could see that the conversation was getting nowhere. 'Paul, there are some things that are minor, and don't have any great meanin' or significance, like the Ariel you were workin' on today. Sure, I could've charged the owner for every minute you spent tryin' to fix it, but it could've had some unintended long-term costs. I could've lost a customer and he could've spread it around that I'd ripped him off. Who's being fair then?'

Paul didn't reply.

'As Mike said, there're swings and roundabouts. It could've cost me today, but I could reap the benefits tomorrow. If I hadn't stood up for you today at the sandwich shop, that could've meant that you'd lose confidence in me. *That* was a price I *wasn't* prepared ta pay.'

After the table had been cleared and the dishes had been washed and put away, Paul turned on the television, while the old mechanic booted up his laptop. He went straight to eBay and located the items that he had placed bids on. Five items had finished – he was successful on three and missed out on two – and he had to increase his bid on several others. He searched for alternate items to replace the two he was unsuccessful with and placed a bid on them. He then contacted the vendors of the items he had successfully bid for and arranged payment and delivery.

The old mechanic was not a great fan of on-line auctions, but he did concede that it was probably the cheapest method of buying spare parts. He just hoped that they were in as good condition as the photographs and descriptions suggested. When he had finished, he joined Paul in front of the box in the lounge room.

'Wha d'ya been doin'?' asked Paul.

'Puttin' bids on the parts for your bike.'

'But I thought you did that the other day.'

'I did, but I had to increase my bid for some and find other parts I missed out on.'

'Why don't ya just buy the parts from a shop?'

'Price! eBay's usually cheaper than you'd pay retail, but you have to know how much parts normally cost, because there are sharks out there.'

'When d'ya think we'll be able to start fixin' it?'

'If I'm successful on all the bids, I reckon we might be able to start the end of next week.'

'How much is it gonna cost?'

'I'll tell you next week.'

Chapter 9

ON THE ROAD AGAIN

The three mechanics assembled for work the following morning. It was Friday, and usually the busiest day of the week as customers clambered to have their precious machines ready for riding over the weekend. Of course, those who planned ahead and booked their bikes in readiness were given priority. But there was always one or two who left it to the last minute. The standing policy was: "Poor planning on your part does not necessarily constitute an emergency on ours."

But regardless of the workload, planned or otherwise, the three men always commenced work with a cuppa. There was the usual banter about work and, being a Friday, plans for the weekend.

Almost as an afterthought, Michael advised, 'By the way, Katie's comin' back to work on Mond'y.'

The old mechanic nearly spilled his tea in his surprise. 'What's she gonna do with the bub?'

'She's gonna bring him too. He sleeps most of the day, so he prob'ly won't notice too much. And he'll be in the office with her, so she'll be right there with him if he wakes up.'

'We'll hafta keep the noise down, but,' added Paul.

'But what am I gonna do?' whined the old mechanic. 'I'm gonna be without a job.'

'You c'n go back to doin' what you're best at – restoring classic motorcycles – Emeritus Mechanic,' Michael advised smiling.

'And here I was, just gettin' used to bein' a shiny bum!'
Everyone laughed.

Katie's return to work was seamless. The workload was so high in the workshop that the old mechanic had little time to search for another classic machine to restore, let alone commence a restoration. But that suited everyone; more work meant more money coming in to the business.

It would take three more weeks to assemble all the parts needed to refurbish the accident damaged Triumph Bonneville, and a further month before the old mechanic and Paul found time to commence the work. Being a personal motorcycle, it remained at the bottom of the list of priorities in the workshop. Nevertheless, in his spare time, Paul had already started to strip the machine of the damaged parts, as well as those items that made it illegal for him. Even though the bike now technically belonged to Paul, it would be forever known as "Kieran's Bonnie."

The list of damaged parts was relatively small. The left-side of the tank had been dented and scratched, the glass in the headlight smashed, the handlebars bent, and the controls and indicators on the left side either bent or broken. However, the frame, forks, wheels, seat and the entire right-hand side survived undamaged. After the dirt had been washed off and the damaged parts removed, Paul surveyed the machine. He rued the fact he could not legally ride it as a P plater, but no amount of arguing could persuade the old mechanic to change his mind. Still, he reasoned, a 650 was better than a "no"-50.

The old mechanic had sent the tank, front and rear mudguards and the left-hand side-cover to the paint shop in Tamworth for repair and repainting. Having already painted these same items the previous year for their last owner, the paint shop proprietor was familiar with their history and the tragic outcome of its last ride. He did not ask the old mechanic about the new owner – it was none of his concern.

Other than the larger capacity pistons and barrels, and bigger valves, the old mechanic was unsure what other modifications had been made to the motor. The quickest option would be to ring up John Traeghier and ask him. But after their last conversation, he thought better of it. So once Paul had removed the head and barrels, they examined everything carefully. They found that the cylinder head had been ported and polished, with hardened valve seats, new guides and heavy-duty springs. There was also a lumpier camshaft.

If the bike was to revert to being a 650 permanently, the head, valves and camshaft would all need to be replaced with standard items. But with Paul's stated intention of making it a 750 again once he was on his unrestricted licence, the added costs would be unjustifiable. So the two men left things as they were, hoping they would be able to get the motor running properly with the "hot" head and cam.

The old mechanic was able to salvage a matching pair of 1¼ inch Amal Monobloc carburettors from a wreck to replace the pair of Mikuni CV carbies. While larger than standard, they could be able to be adapted to suit the modified head. All they would need was a gasket set, which included the necessary gaskets, seals, needles and jetting screws. The bottom of the motor, as well as the gearbox needed no work done to them, except a check of torque tensioning and a change of oil. All the bearings were as good as new.

The left-hand side reverse-cone stainless steel megaphone exhaust bore the scars of having been dropped in the gravel. However, once it had been polished, the scratches became almost invisible, and nearly matched the other unscratched exhaust. What is more, there was every chance that one or both sides would kiss the ground more than once again in their next life.

Normally, the motor and chassis of a classic bike that was over 50 years old would bear the telltale signs of having been worked on over the years, with rusty nuts and screws with rounded corners and butchered heads. But all of the fasteners on Kieran's Bonnie were still as they might have been when they first left the factory, having been replaced with shiny stainless steel items when the bike was restored.

Paul wanted to do the restoration work himself, as much as possible. He spent all of his weekends and after hours during the week, when he did not have other chores to do. Michael and the old mechanic admired his work ethic, not to mention the quality of his work. Over the subsequent weeks, his skills as a mechanic and his knowledge about repairing all types of classic British motorcycles grew exponentially. Neither the old mechanic nor Michael regretted their decision to employ him – well, not yet anyway.

The October long-weekend loomed large. Michael and Katie would be celebrating their first wedding anniversary. But it was also a date that brought back sad memories.

The three mechanics and Katie gathered for their morning cuppa on the Friday before the long-weekend.

'You two got plans for the weekend?' asked the old mechanic.

'Yeah, we're going down to Coffs to celebrate our first annivers'ry,' announced Michael with a glint in his eye. 'Oh, that reminds me, we'll be leavin' around lunchtime, if that's alright with you.'

'Mike, you're the boss. You c'n leave whenever you please. Just take care on the roads, and remember, it's double demerits all weekend.'

'Yeah, I will.'

'You mean we will,' added Katie. 'I'll be driving too. Speaking of long-weekends, you know this is the weekend that Lilly and Kieran were supposed to be getting married.'

There was silence for a few moments, each one lost in their own thoughts. Eventually, the old mechanic asked, 'Have you seen Lilly lately? I wonder how she's copin'.'

'I haven't seen her since the funeral. I don't even know if she knows we have baby Kieran. I tried calling her mobile, but it just rings out.'

'What about Facebook?' asked Michael.

Katie shook her head. 'She hasn't posted anything since before the accident.'

There was a pause again before Paul asked, 'What's Facebook?'

Michael smiled. 'It's a social media website that you can personalise and post comments and photos. Your friends can do the same on your page and you can do it on theirs. You c'n see it on your smartphone, tablet or computer.'

'I ain't got a smartphone, tablet or computer.'

Michael whipped out his iPhone and quickly showed him his Facebook page.

After viewing it and reading some of the posts, Paul responded, 'I don't know why you'd wanna do that? I can't see the point.'

Katie cut in. 'It's for keeping in touch with people. That's why it's called social media.'

'But I thought that's what telephones were for.'

Everybody laughed.

'Welcome to the twenty-first century Paul.'

The day passed quickly. After Michael and Katie left during the lunch break, the old mechanic and Paul worked furiously to get the customer bikes finished before it was time to lock up. The older man was exhausted from the effort. It had been a full-on week, culminating in the busiest of days.

At times like this, the old mechanic wished he could just go home and put his feet up while his missus prepared dinner. Fortunately, Paul could sense that his landlord come housemate was ready to collapse, and volunteered to cook – it would be his first opportunity to demonstrate his culinary skills in the kitchen.

The old mechanic had already defrosted sufficient steak, sausages, chops, bacon strips and lambs fry in preparation for the evening meal, so all Paul needed to do was cook them. But instead of the usual bland mixed grill that the old mechanic had planned, Paul marinated the meat in an assortment of spices to give the meal an additional hit of flavour.

After he had finished eating, the old mechanic gave a satisfied burp. 'Pardon me. You said you could cook, but you didn't say how good you were. That was absolutely delicious Paul. You c'n cook tomorrow too if ya like?'

Paul grinned. 'You should try my marinated baked witchetty grubs.'

'Umm … ah … I think I'll stick to beef, lamb, chicken and pork, thanks.'

'Oh, come on George, where's ya sense of adventure?'

'When it comes ta food, chicken chow mein is about as adventurous as I like ta get.'

Paul started to clear the table. 'What're we doin' on the weekend?'

'The grass needs mowin' and I've got a load of washin' ta do. I also need to get some groceries.'

'I'll do the grass if you do the washin', an' we c'n do the shoppin' t'gether. I need ta get a few things too.'

'Whaddya need?'

'I wanna get some clothes, an' if I'm gonna do some more cookin', I need some more spices.'

'Just make sure the spices don't make it *too* spicy. An' no witchetty grubs, okay?'

Paul smiled. 'The supermarket don't stock witchetty grubs, yet.'

'Good.'

When all the chores had been completed and the shopping done, Paul made his way to the workshop to continue the restoration of Kieran's Bonnie. He found the gasket set that they had ordered and set about servicing the twin Amal carburettors. When that was completed, he installed them on the engine.

The disappointment he had initially felt at turning the motorcycle back into a 650 was being slowly replaced by the growing excitement that it would soon be finished. With the motor now complete, he would be able to fit the controls, indicators and lights, and refit the instruments that had been removed when the handlebars were replaced. The newly painted tank, mudguards and left-hand side-cover were sitting in a box, having been retrieved from the paint shop the previous week.

Paul had already checked the wheels to ensure they remained true. He had only ever laced a spoked rim once during his TAFE course, and wasn't confident of doing it again, so he was pleased that this skill would not be required now. He fitted the front and rear mudguards, taking care that he did not mark the freshly painted items, and both wheels. The chain was coated in a sticky grease, and made a mess of his hands when he eased it over the rear sprocket. Once the tank was installed and plumbed in, all that was required was the filling of the oil tank and the fuel tank. He would leave tuning the carburettors until either Michael or the old mechanic was around for advice.

Excitement filled the workshop the following Tuesday. Katie and Michael had had a most enjoyable weekend. Baby Kieran had started sleeping right though the night, giving them a much needed rest. The traffic to Armidale and down the Waterfall Way to Bellingen and home again had been relatively light, and the weather was brilliant sunshine every day. What more could they have wanted?

Paul proudly showed off the Triumph Bonneville 650 cc T120 that was, to all intents and purposes, finished.

'Have you taken it for a ride yet?' asked Michael.

'Nah, I haven't started it. I need someone to gimme a hand tunin' the carbies but. An' it needs a battery too.'

'Isn't there a spare battery in the storeroom?' asked the old mechanic.

'There's a 6-volt there, but the Bonnie needs a 12.'

'I'll look after that,' said Katie.

With the shorter week and the high workload, it was not until Friday afternoon that Michael and Paul had time to get the tune of the carburettors sorted. After installing the battery, and filling the tanks with fluids, the new owner of Kieran's Bonnie turned on the tap, tickled the carburettors, and gave the kick-starter a prod. It coughed, but did not start.

'Make sure the float bowl's full, then bring the piston to the top of its compression stroke before giving it a decent kick,' Michael advised.

Paul followed the instructions. This time the engine fired, with a loud bark from the twin unbaffled exhausts. He twisted the throttle several times before allowing it to idle. It was running a little roughly, suggesting that the carburettors would still require some fine adjustments, but at least it was running.

'Gee it's loud,' shouted Michael, his hands momentarily covering his ears.

"Aye, wha' d'ja say? I can't hear ya,' said Paul with a grin from ear to ear.

Chapter 10

FILIAL COMMITMENTS

The old mechanic did not see much of Paul all day Saturday. The Triumph Bonneville was still registered in the name of its previous owner as a "LAMS" approved motorcycle. So Paul lined up at 8:00 am for the Tamworth RMS Office to open at 8:30, with the paperwork completed and sufficient funds to pay the stamp duty and registration transfer costs, to get the bike registered in his name.

When his number was called, Paul approached the customer service officer at the counter. She eyed him suspiciously before examining his documentation. She had never before had a young Aboriginal apply to have a classic motorcycle registered in his name.

'Is this your motorbike?' she asked.

'Yeah.'

'Where did you get it from?'

'Me boss give it to me.'

'How much did you pay for it?'

'Nothin'.'

The customer service officer looked closely at the signature on the transfer documentation. 'This doesn't look like the signature of the previous owner. Who signed it?'

'The last owner got killed. That's his ol' man's signature.'

Not satisfied with Paul's answers, she took the forms to her supervisor. An officious-looking fat man wearing thick glasses waddled over to the counter to speak with Paul.

'Is this your motorbike son?'

'Yessir.' Paul felt immediately intimidated.

'Did you purchase it from the previous owner?'

Paul was getting frustrated, faced with another round of questions, but he did his best to remain civil. He let out a sigh before replying. 'The last guy who owned it got killed. His ol' man give it to my boss, and me boss give it to me. I didn't pay for it, but I did fix it up and got it goin' again.'

'Don't get testy with me son, I'm only tryin' to do my job. Now who's this boss of yours?'

'George Edwards, Classic Bike Repairs and Service.' Paul retrieved a business card from his wallet with the old mechanic's telephone number on it and passed it to the official. 'Give him a call; his number's there. He'll tell ya I ain't lyin'.'

'Alright, take a seat. We'll call you when we're ready.'

The supervisor waited fifteen minutes before he rang the old mechanic who gave him the confirmation that the transfer of ownership was legitimate. But the petty bureaucrat was not going to let the young Aboriginal mechanic have any easy time of it. So, he let him wait for a further 40 minutes before giving the customer service officer the authority to approve the transfer. Mercifully, Paul was none the wiser and just assumed that the processing of the transfer took that amount of time.

It seemed that passive racism was endemic in every strata of Australian society.

At the insistence of the old mechanic, baffles had been installed inside the twin megaphone exhaust pipes, so the noise they emitted as he rode off from the RMS Office was somewhat muted compared to when he started the machine in the workshop the previous afternoon. They would now be less likely to attract unwanted attention as well.

With a jacket, jeans, gloves and a full-face helmet, Paul was as anonymous as any other rider could be. Unless someone got close enough to see his face through the clear visor, there would be no way of determining the colour of his skin, or that he was Aboriginal. But nobody did. He was delighted when some other riders acknowledged him by raising a finger as he rode past. He had never experienced that kind of camaraderie before.

When he arrived home late in the afternoon, the old mechanic was waiting for him. Paul's face was beaming when he removed his helmet, but not for long.

'How was the ride?'

'T'riffic.'

'Where'd ya go?'

'All over the place.'

'Did you have any trouble with the bike?'

'Of course not.' He smiled. 'I done a good job restorin' it.'

'Umm … your Uncle Danny came by. He wants ta see ya.'

Paul was immediately serious. 'Did 'e say why?'

'No, only that it was important.'

Uncle Danny Stewart did not usually make social calls. Something must have happened, but what, and to whom, Paul would have to wait to find out.

When he had parked the Triumph in the workshop, he rang the home number of the Kamilaroi Elder. At first it was engaged. He waited a few minutes and tried again. This time, the telephone was answered on the second ring. After his initial greeting, Paul was silent as he listened. Some time later he grunted his farewells and hung up the receiver.

The old mechanic was busy preparing dinner. He looked up expectantly when the call ended, but Paul said nothing and left the kitchen for his bedroom. Ten minutes later, the old mechanic found him sitting on the edge of his bed.

'Dinner'll be ready soon.'

Paul shook his head. 'I ain't that hungry.'

'I take it the news wasn't great.'

Paul shook his head. 'It's me mum.' A tear trickled down his left cheek, glistening in the pale light of the globe beside the bed.

'Is she alright?'

'She topped herself las' night.'

The old mechanic was shocked at the news, and the almost matter-of-fact manner in which it was delivered. He sat down on the bed and put his arm around the shoulder of the young Aboriginal mechanic. 'I'm so sorry Paul. Is there anything we can do?'

Paul shook his head again. 'Nah ... it's too late now.' He sobbed as the older man held him tightly, his mind swirling with the twin emotions of guilt and sadness.

The old mechanic suddenly remembered dinner. He jumped up and rushed back to the kitchen just in time to take the stew from the stove. He dished up the meal before returning to the bedroom.

'You can't do anything for her now Paul. Come and have a bite to eat. You'll need strength for tomorrow.'

Paul was quieter than usual during the meal, and excused himself straight after the table had been cleared. Later that evening, when the old mechanic retired for the night, he could hear soft crying coming from the younger man's bedroom. He thought about going in, but decided to let him grieve in private. Sometimes crying was best.

The old mechanic was unsure how Paul would be the following morning. So, it was to his surprise that the young Aboriginal was back to his bright and cheerful self.

'How'd you sleep?'

'Like a log.'

'Do you know when the funeral is yet?'

'Nah, Uncle Danny'll let me know. We hafta wait 'til all the family arrives. It could be this week or nex', or it might even be nex' month.'

The old mechanic was surprised. 'Really?'

'Yeah, fun'rals are always big family events. I'm really lookin' forward to seein' everyone again, 'specially me sisters. I don't wanna go to the wake but. Everyone us'lly gets pissed an' then the fightin' starts.'

'Do you want me to come with you?'

'What, to the fun'ral?'

'Yeah.'

Paul eyed the old mechanic doubtfully. 'You don't hafta, ya know. I'll be alright but.'

'I want to.'

The Aboriginal mechanic beamed. 'Thanks George.'

'Make sure I get to meet your sisters.'

'Of course. They'll prob'ly wanna meet you anyhow.'

Both Michael and Katie expressed sadness when they heard the news the following Monday morning, and surprise when they learned the cause of death. It transpired that Paul's mother died of a drug overdose, but whether intentional or accidental was yet to be determined. All three of his colleagues were aware of the reasons for Paul not wishing to reside at the family home, but they were sad for his loss just the same.

'Do you want some time off?' asked Katie. 'You should be entitled to Compassionate Leave or something.' She had received Compassionate Leave from her employer when her mother and partner had died and just assumed everyone should receive some time off when a close relative passed away.

'Wha' do I need time off for?'

'I don't know. Arrange the funeral perhaps.'

'Me sisters're doin' that. I need time off ta go ta the service but.'

'What say we close the workshop and all of us go?' suggested Michael. He looked to his father-in-law for agreement.

'I was going anyway Mike, but I think that's a great idea. We just need to let our customers know.'

Paul had not expected such overwhelming support. He did not know what to say, except 'Thanks everyone.'

With the move away from the traditional thanksgiving services of the past, most contemporary funerals are more about the celebration of the life of the deceased person. However, there was little in the life of Lynette Suzanne Tracey worth celebrating. A member of the "Stolen Generation", she was raised in a Catholic Girls' Home where she was molested by the local parish priest. At 14, she went to work on a sheep station west of Narrabri as a house girl where she was brutally treated by the owner's wife. When she became pregnant after being raped by the Leading Hand, she was sent back to Tamworth to stay with a cousin. She became involved in drugs, and subsequently, alcohol, courtesy of one of her many partners. Four more children arrived, with Paul being the youngest.

Paul's sisters had trouble agreeing on the type of funeral they would give their mother; whether a religious funeral in a church, or a traditional service held in the open air. Eventually they compromised, after the intervention of Uncle Danny Stewart. They used elements of the catholic burial rites by a priest as well as elements from the traditional funeral ceremony. The first part was held in the funeral home chapel and the second part at the graveside.

The old mechanic, Michael, Katie and baby Kieran stood out as the only white faces in the crowd of mourners. Paul kept close by, introducing them to his sisters, their partners, and his many uncles, aunts and cousins. Some were suspicious of the white fellas, but mellowed somewhat after hearing that they were Paul's friends and had provided him with work and accommodation, even if they were unsure why he would not want to live with his own mob.

The funeral was unlike anything that Paul's colleagues had ever experienced. There was much public display of grief, with his sisters leading the wailing and crying. While not wishing to be too judgemental, Katie was grateful that she had not been born into Aboriginal culture. She was relieved when they left the chapel and attended the graveside for the traditional ceremony.

The contrast between the traditional ceremony and funerals that the three colleagues had previously experienced could not have been more stark. Numerous men were armed with clapping sticks and pairs of boomerangs used to tap out a beat, while two others played didgeridoos. Men and women chanted or sang songs that lasted from mere seconds to several minutes each, all the while dancing to the beat.

The singing, chanting, playing and dancing went on for over half an hour. The old mechanic, Michael and Katie were fascinated by the spectacle. Eventually the priest laid the body to rest and gave the benediction, signalling that the funeral had come to an end. Now the drinking could start in earnest.

Several of Paul's cousins began pressuring him to stay on and get drunk with them, but he knew the likely outcome, and begged their indulgence. He kissed each of his sisters goodbye and left the funeral in the back seat of Michael and Katie's car. It was a tight squeeze with the baby capsule on one side, Katie in the middle and Paul behind the driver. It certainly helped that neither were particularly large.

When they were clear of the cemetery, Katie asked, 'Are your funerals all like that?'

Paul smiled. 'What, black fella fun'rals?'

'Yeah. I've never experienced anything like that before.'

'That's a first for me too,' advised the old mechanic.

'Ditto,' said Michael.

'It all depends,' informed Paul. 'If he was brung up a white fella, the fun'ral's jus' like one a yours. But if he's raised a black fella, the fun'ral's uzh'ly more tradit'nal.'

'There seemed to be elements of both black and white in your mum's funeral,' suggested Michael.

'That's 'cos me sisters couldn't agree. The two oldest ones wanted a church fun'ral, but the younger ones wanted a tradit'nal one.'

'I think having elements from both cultures is a good idea, especially if it brings together two opposing sides,' added Michael.

Paul smiled. 'Jus' as long as they pick the best elements, an' not the worst but.'

'Did you have a say?' asked Katie.

'What, in the fun'ral? Nah, I didn't care. Mum wasn't real religious. Me oldest sister was but. Did ya see how many kids she's got?'

Chapter 11

GHOSTLY APPEARANCE

The afternoon was far spent when the car arrived back at the workshop. An express courier delivering parts arrived at the same time, so Michael opened up to accept the items. But it was too late to start any work, so he and Katie departed for home, leaving behind the old mechanic and Paul.

After changing out of their funeral attire, Paul returned to the kitchen ready to prepare dinner. With more than the usual amount of time available, he decided it was time to show off the culinary skills he had picked up in prison in making a Moroccan lamb with couscous.

The old mechanic loved lamb, and he loved stews, but he had not eaten a decent lamb stew since Katie got married and moved out. His own attempts paled in comparison. However, he had never tasted Moroccan spices, let alone couscous, so he looked forward to dinner with equal parts excitement and apprehension.

The aromas from the stew bubbling away on the stove filled the small cottage, and made his mouth water. The anticipation he felt was not betrayed by the resulting meal which the old mechanic found delicious.

'I think you've missed your calling.'

'Wha' d'ya mean?'

'Did ya ever consider becomin' a chef?'

Paul smiled. 'Nah, I cook 'cos I love eatin'. I think I'd stop enjoyin' cookin' if I had ta do it for a livin'.'

'Well, I'm more than happy to relinquish my position as chief cook, and revert to chief bottle washer.'

'An' pot scraper,' added Paul.

'Yeah, that too.'

'The only thing I don't like 'bout cookin' is the cleanin' up after but.'

'Well, if you're happy to keep cooking meals like this, I'm more than happy to do the cleaning up after you. Deal?'

'Deal.'

As they were finishing their meal, out of the blue, Paul asked, 'Wha' dya think happens ta people when they kark it?'

The old mechanic had not anticipated the question, and was not really prepared for a deep and meaningful answer. 'I dunno. Some people believe in heaven and hell; some in purgatory. Some believe this life is all there is. Wha' da *you* think?'

Paul shrugged his shoulders. 'Our culture says everyone has a spirit. An' when ya die, the spirits go ta the Land of Eternal Dreamin'. But not everyone; some c'n get lost on the way.'

'You wondering about ya mum?'

'Yeah, I s'pose.'

'Why don'cha ask your Uncle Danny? He might have a better idea.'

'We talked about it once when I was gettin' initiated, but I didn't really un'erstand it but.'

'We often don't understand things until they start to have personal relevance for us.'

'D'you b'lieve in spirits?'

'What, like evil spirits?'

'Yeah, but good spirits too.'

'No, not really. I certainly don't believe in ghosts.'

'Wha' about the evil spirit in Kieran's Bonnie?'

The old mechanic did not wish to deny the existence of some kind of negative force that seemed to have caused the series of mishaps that included his own heart attack. But neither did he want to affirm that an evil spirit was the cause.

'Look Paul, I struggle to understand the physical world around us. I'd rather leave the spirit world to those who are so inclined.'

'I wasn't askin' if ya un'erstand spirits, jus' if ya b'lieve in 'em.'

'Umm, I think it's time I did the washin' up.'

Paul had not thought much about his mother since he was released from prison, and even after he had been informed of her untimely death, he had not thought much about her. But after attending her funeral and being questioned by his sisters about his living arrangements, he was reminded that he had virtually turned his back on her, indeed that is what some of his mob had accused him of doing. While he had already rationalised to his own satisfaction the reasons for not wanting to return to the family home, Paul nonetheless started to have guilt feelings about whether he could have prevented her death. Later that night, he had difficulty getting to sleep.

'Paulie, Paulie.'

Paul felt a chill in the room. 'Who's that?'

'Why didn't ya come 'ome? I was waitin' for ya.'

'Who is it?'

'Why did ya hafta turn ya back on ya dear mama? I needed ya ta come 'ome.'

'I couldn't come home mama. I needed ta turn me life around. You knew that.'

'I'm still waitin' for ya Paulie. Come 'ome.'

'I can't mama … I can't.'

Paul sat up in bed, his heart racing. He switched on the bedside lamp, but he was alone in the room.

The old mechanic opened the door to his cry. 'Are you alright Paul?'

'She was here.'

'Who was?'

'Me mum ... she was right here.'

He looked around the room. 'There's no-one else here Paul. I think you were havin' a nightmare.'

'No ... she was here ... she said she was waitin' for me.'

'Paul, no-one else has been here. I didn't hear anyone else talkin' except you. You were dreamin'. Now go back to sleep.'

Paul was certain that his mother had been there with him in his room. She had been so real for him that she could only have been a ghost. He tried to sleep, but spent the night tossing and turning, continually expecting his mother to reappear.

At about 6:00 am the following morning he emerged from his bedroom looking tired and drawn from a lack of sleep. He visited the toilet, and then the bathroom, where he splashed cold water on his face in a futile attempt to make himself more awake, before filling the basin with warm water to shave. Paul would have preferred to go back to bed, but work beckoned.

The old mechanic found him sitting at the kitchen table with his head cradled in his arms. 'You look terrible.'

'Yeah, I di'n't sleep much.'

'Did ya mother's ghost reappear?'

'Nah, you musta scared her off.'

The old mechanic almost said, or it was just a dream, just as I said, but he kept his peace. Paul did not appear to be in the mood to get into a heavy discussion that morning. 'Why don'cha go back ta bed?'

'I gotta start work soon.'

'You don't look like you're in any fit state to be workin' today. In fact, you're more likely to have an accident if you're tired 'cause you haven't slept. I'll just tell Mike you're not feelin' well. He'll be okay about it.'

'But what if she comes back?'

'Who, your mum? We'll worry about that when it happens.'

Both Michael and Katie were concerned when the old mechanic informed them that Paul was not feeling well and would be spending the day in bed. He did not tell them about the ghostly appearance. That could wait until the young Aboriginal was able to defend himself.

Despite the light coming from his bedroom window, or maybe because of it, Paul slept fitfully, right up until almost lunchtime. He woke feeling hungry, but refreshed. Having skipped breakfast, he did not wish to miss lunch. After quickly dressing in his overalls, he left the house and made his way to the workshop.

'How're ya feelin'?' asked Michael.

'Much better now thanks. I'm starvin' but. Has anyone gone to get the lunches yet?'

'I'm just about to go,' said Katie as she emerged from her office. 'Do you want me to get you something?'

'Yes please missus.'

'Call me Katie please Paul. Missus sounds a bit too formal.'

Paul blushed.

When Katie returned with the lunches, everyone gathered together and sat around the small table with their sandwiches as the jug boiled for a cuppa.

Not content to let sleeping dogs lie, or sleeping ghosts either for that matter, the old mechanic asked, 'So Paul, did she make a reappearance?'

'Who?' asked Michael and Katie together.

'Nah, I think there was too much light in the room.'

'Who are you talking about?' asked Katie.

'Me mum.'

'But you buried her yesterday,' said Michael.

'Her ghost musta foll'ed us back. She came ta me bedroom las' night.'

Michael and Katie looked at each other and then at the old mechanic. He shrugged his shoulders.

'I reckon he was havin' a nightmare, but he was adamant he saw her ghost.'

'It was her ghost. Why else would the room have been so cold?'

Michael and Katie looked at the old mechanic for the answer. 'I didn't think it was all that cold.'

'It could've been a ghost,' affirmed Katie. 'Did she say anything?'

'Yeah, she said she was waitin' for me.'

'Did she say where?'

'Oh come on Katie.' The old mechanic was starting to get annoyed. 'It was nothin' but a dream … a nightmare. He went to bed thinkin' about his mum, and then he dreamed about her; that's all, end of story.'

'But …'

The old mechanic raised his voice as he declared, 'There *is* no damn ghost in my house.' He slammed his enamel cup down on the table and stormed off out of the workshop.

It had been a long time since anyone had seen the old mechanic lose his temper. Michael was about to follow his father-in-law outside, but Katie placed her hand on his arm to stop him.

'I'll go.'

The old mechanic stopped at the end of the laneway. Katie followed him, stopping several paces behind.

'Daddy.'

He turned around, 'Hello sweetheart.'

'What are you angry for?'

The old mechanic seemed lost for words. Eventually he shook his head and said, 'I'm just sick of all this talk about evil spirits and ghosts. There's no such thing. It's all jus' a bunch o' crap.'

'But why are you angry?'

He did not reply.

'Everyone has their own beliefs. Some people believe in God or gods, some people in angels and spirits, and others in fairies, goblins and elves. Everyone has the right to believe in whatever they want to.'

'That's fine. I'm happy to accept that. But what happens when it impacts on others? What happens when it impacts on me?'

'What do you mean?'

'Well, we've already had one damn smoking ceremony to get rid o' the evil spirit in Kieran's Bonnie, what happens if Paul wants to hold another one to get rid of his mother's ghost out of my own house?'

'Has he said that?'

'Not yet.'

Katie smiled and touched his arm. 'Daddy, why are you angry about something that hasn't happened, and might never happen?'

The old mechanic did not reply.

'Paul's probably feeling guilty over his mother's death; about whether or not he could've done anything to prevent it. His guilt is most likely mixed up with the grieving process. Just give him some time; he'll get over it.'

The old mechanic smiled and put his arm around Katie's shoulders. 'Yeah, I s'pose you're right. You know who you sound like?'

'No, who?'

'Me.'

'You were a good teacher.'

Later that evening over dinner, Paul said, 'I'm sorry if you were upset 'bout me sayin' I saw me mum's ghost.'

'Nah, that's alright. I'm sorry too. I shouldn't have reacted the way I did.'

'Is it alright if I call Uncle Danny?'

'Yeah, sure. Just don't ask him to perform a smokin' ceremony in your bedroom.'

'Nah, o' course not. He might burn the house down.'

'Yeah, that's what I was afraid of.'

Chapter 12

SKIN DEEP

The weather was warming up. Even though it was still only spring, afternoon temperatures were already exceeding 30 degrees celsius on some days. There had even been a number of bushfires in the nearby State Forests that were believed started by electrical storms. The unseasonably hot temperatures did not augur well for a mild and comfortable summer. But at least the warmer weather meant an increased number of people riding motorcycles. Even riders of classic machines preferred to ride in warm weather over cold.

When the three mechanics and Katie gathered for their mid-morning smoko, the old mechanic found Michael and Katie in earnest discussion.

'What's up?'

'I rang Mrs Henderson after I got to work this morning.'

The name did not register with the old mechanic, so he shook his head and shrugged his shoulders.

Katie continued. 'She's Lilly's mother.'

The name suddenly registered. 'Oh yeah. Did she tell you how Lilly was?'

'Yeah, she's in the James Fletcher Hospital in Newcastle.'

'What happened? Did she have an accident?' The old mechanic was instantly concerned.

'The James Fletcher is a psychiatric hospital. Lilly had a mental breakdown.'

'Oh no, poor kid. Is she alright?'

'I don't know. Mrs Henderson was in tears when I spoke to her, so I couldn't get a lot of sense out of her. But apparently Mr Henderson's in denial.'

'I'm not surprised. I thought he was a bit of a dipstick when I met him that day we went to the park for Kieran's baptism.'

'Why don'cha try an' call the hospital,' suggested Michael, 'they might let you talk to her.'

'I did after I called Mrs Henderson, but they said she couldn't come to the phone. They also said she wasn't able to see any visitors; just immediate family.'

'Sounds like solit'ry confinement,' commented Paul.

'Thankfully, the days of lockin' people up in padded cells and keepin' 'em in straight jackets is long past,' advised the old mechanic, 'as they should be.'

'The trouble is,' added Michael, 'a lot of those who, years ago, would've been locked up in mental hospitals or institutions, are now locked up in prisons.'

'How do you know that?'

'I saw it in a doco on the tele.'

'Yeah, we sure had a few psychos in our gaol. But most o' them went crazy 'cause of crack or ganja,' advised Paul.

'It doesn't matter how people become mentally unwell,' commented Katie, 'prison isn't the right place for them.'

The old mechanic could see where the discussion was heading, so he decided to change the subject. 'I think it's time we got back to work.'

The days were passing quickly as everyone was busy with the large number of classic motorcycles in the workshop for repairs and service. Katie was kept especially busy as the business had started to stock spare parts for sale to those enthusiasts who preferred to perform their own maintenance tasks. While the range of parts was limited to the higher turnover items for the more popular models, the service was proving popular.

Baby Kieran was growing and had started making an appearance during breaks. While both father and grandfather were often unable to hold him for fear of soiling his clothes with grease from their overalls, they were happy to assist with feeding duties, particularly now that he was sitting up and had started on solids.

Paul, for his part, had become intrigued with Michael and Katie's relationship and how they related to others in the workshop, both work colleagues and customers. Growing up in a dysfunctional family, he had no positive role models from whom to learn. He had only ever known violence and abuse, both physical and verbal, between individuals and within families, often fuelled by alcohol and drugs.

So to see a man and a woman who clearly loved one another, display respect and courtesy to each other, and indeed to everyone else, was truly fascinating for him. He began to wonder how much more different his own life would have been if he had been born into a more loving and nurturing family environment, even if he did not think about it in those exact terms.

Even though Paul's surname was Saunders, he had no recollection of ever having met anyone who shared his name, and no-one claiming to be his father was at his mother's funeral. There had been several "fathers" over the years, but most of them had been violent to him and/or to his mother and sisters. Each sister had a different surname, but whether that was because they each had a different father or because his mother chose to name them that way was also a mystery to him.

Paul had not thought much about girls in the past, let alone getting into a relationship with one. But seeing how Michael and Katie's marriage was working, started to get him thinking. All he needed to do was to find a girl, but who, and where?

One evening over dinner, he questioned the old mechanic. 'How did Mike and Katie meet?'

'Umm, well, they'd seen each other when Mike came to work for me, but I think they came to know each other when he was the first on the scene after Katie's former partner was killed in a car accident. Mike gave first aid to her, and so he became her "accidental hero". They started going out together after that. Why do you ask?'

'Oh, just thinkin'.'

'What, about them?'

'Nah, not really.'

Paul dropped his gaze and blushed. His face would have turned scarlet if it was not so dark.

'She's pretty special, isn't she?'

'Yeah, but she's taken.'

The old mechanic smiled when he realised what Paul was getting at. 'You wanna meet someone like Katie?'

'Yeah, sort of. I don' wanna white girl but.'

'What does it matter? Colour's only skin deep. Remember our first meeting? It's not the colour of the skin that's important.'

Paul continued the line. 'Yeah, I know, it's whether or not you c'n do the job. But we ain't talkin' about work here, we're talkin' 'bout relationships.'

The old mechanic put down his eating implements. 'You're right Paul, that's exactly what we're talking about. You, me, Mike and Katie, young Kieran, even our customers, are all in a relationship. Sure it's not a marriage as such, but it's still a relationship. Doing the work of a motorcycle mechanic is more than just about being good with spanners. It's just as much how you relate to your work colleagues and to your customers.

'What's more, Mike and Katie aren't in a relationship just because they're both white fellas. They're married because they love each other and want to spend the rest of their lives together – colour had nothin' to do with it. If you want to find someone to form a relationship with, don't just restrict your choices to the black community.'

'A white girl wouldn't be interested in a black fella but.'

The old mechanic smiled. 'Who says? If that was the case, there wouldn't be *any* mixed marriages. But we both know there are. It's not the colour of the skin that's important, it's what's deep down inside. Now, if you were *only* interested in looking for a black girl, that's different.'

Paul thought for a moment. 'I s'pose I don't really care – black or white – I jus' wanna meet someone as nice as Katie.'

The old mechanic thought to himself, yeah, that makes two of us. 'Why don'cha call your Uncle Danny? Ask him if he knows of any social events for Aboriginal young people. You might meet someone there.'

'A lotta times they jus' turn inta drinkin' contests but, an' then the fightin' starts.'

'It doesn't hafta be, and you could always leave if it does.'

'Where did you meet your missus, you know, Katie's mum?'

'We met at a church picnic in the days when we both used to go to church. Yeah, well that's another option – you could always start goin' to church.'

'I don't think so.'

'Why not? I think you'll find there's a church in South Tamworth that caters specifically for Aborigines.'

'Oh, I dunno, I don' wanna get all religious.'

'Well, your choice Paul. I think you should talk to Uncle Danny in the first place. He might have some other ideas. But I'll tell you what – you remember the old saying: "all good things come to those who wait" – if you're waitin' for the right girl to come to you, you'll prob'ly be waitin' a long time. Don't expect someone to come lookin' for you, you gotta get out and start lookin' for yourself.'

Paul had not spoken to Uncle Danny since his mother's funeral, and even then, it was only briefly. He had intended to call him after his mother's spirit appeared to him the night of the funeral, but the urgency waned somewhat when she did not reappear. He wanted to call him about meeting a girl, but he did not know quite what to say.

'Wha' do I say to him?'
'Tell him you're lookin' for a girlfriend.'
'I can't say that.'
'Why not? It's true, isn't it?'
'Yeah, but …'
'Well, tell him you're lookin' for a young lady to form a friendship with.'

Even though what the old mechanic had suggested the second time was, to all intents and purposes, the same as his first suggestion, the way it was expressed was more acceptable to Paul. After the table was cleared and the washing up completed, he called Uncle Danny.

Unbeknownst to Paul, and indeed to most of the younger members of the Tamworth Aboriginal and Torres Strait Islander Community, the Elders performed an unofficial matchmaking service within their mob. Normally, parents or grandparents would contact one of the Elders and ask for advice on finding a suitable partner for their young adult child or grandchild. A social event was then organised where the young people could meet under supervision. However, that was where the service usually ended. Whether or not a relationship was formed was up to the young couple — there was never any coercion, there were certainly no arranged marriages as in some cultures — the Elders, parents and grandparents just allowed nature to take its own course.

It just so happened that Uncle Danny had already organised a barbecue to be held at his home on the following Sunday afternoon. There was to be no "grog", and everyone was expected to bring meat to keep the organiser's costs down. Paul was not told who else would be there, but just to turn up. So he did.

With daylight saving already in operation, the sun did not set in Tamworth until 7:25 pm. Paul arrived home in twilight, riding his Triumph Bonneville. By the time he had parked the bike in the workshop, changed from his riding gear, and joined the old mechanic in front of the television in the lounge room, it was almost half past eight.

'How was the barbie?'

'It was great.'

'Who was there besides Uncle Danny?'

'Ah, lots o' girls.'

The old mechanic smiled. 'Did you meet any nice ones?'

'There was a couple o' really good-lookin' ones — they were half-sisters — daughters of one of Uncle Danny's cousins. They wouldn't let me alone.'

'What were you doin'?'

'I was tryin' ta cook the meat on the barbie.'

'Ah well, there's your problem solved. Women love a man who can do the cookin' for them.'

'Yeah, but I don' know which one to choose.'

'Ah Paul, if only we all had that problem.'

Paul grinned.

The old mechanic continued. 'I'll tell you something else: not only is colour skin deep, so is beauty. Don't just look at the outside, look underneath. The plainest looking people can sometimes be the most beautiful.'

'Yeah, I know. There *was* one other girl. She was a bit ordin'ry lookin', an' real quiet and shy, a bit like what I usta be like. But when she spoke to me, she was real sweet, like bush honey.'

'Do you know who she is?'

'Yeah, Uncle Danny's granddaughter.'

'Do you know her name?'

'Yeah, it's Grace.'

'There you are. If her nature's anything like her name, she might be just the one to go after.'

'An' you know what else?'

'What?'

'She goes to that black fella church in South Tamworth.'

'See, I told ya that was a good place to start lookin'.'

Both men laughed.

Chapter 13

HAUNTED BY HIS PAST

Even though Paul had had no contact with his former gang members – and indeed had made no attempt to do so, now that he had been released from prison – several of them had been trying to make contact with him. It was only after a chance encounter with one of the mourners at his mother's funeral that the gang leader got a pointer regarding his whereabouts.

Paul had not been in a leadership position within the gang. He was more the loyal follower, happy for others to lead and guide in their numerous criminal activities and escapades. But when he had been made to take responsibility for several offences that landed him behind bars, not once but twice, his loyalty became sorely tested. With the support of Uncle Danny, Paul had been able to turn his life around and break the cycle of crime and imprisonment. He had no desire, nor reason, to go back to his old ways and become a gang member again.

None of the gang members lived in the southern suburbs of Tamworth where the workshop was located. Most of the social housing, and subsequently almost all of the gang members, lived in the western suburbs of Taminda and West Tamworth. Yet despite their proximity to the Tamworth Correctional Centre, none of them had visited Paul during his incarceration. Not that he cared much. The lack of interest they showed in him over the previous three and a half years made it easier for him to make the break from them. But now that he had been released from prison, the leader wanted to locate him with a view to bringing him back into the fold, whether he wanted to or not.

The Holden Commodore was once the highest selling car in Australia. It was well suited to the local environment as it would comfortably seat four passengers, plus the driver. It was rugged, had a powerful six- or eight-cylinder motor, parts were cheap and available everywhere, and it was rear wheel drive, meaning it would easily tow a small to medium caravan or boat.

Some of these same features also made it popular with car thieves. Indeed, after adding all of the various models together, it has become the most stolen vehicle in Australia. If they were not taken to be stripped for their spare parts, then they were abused by hoons doing wheelies or used as get away vehicles for robberies, often ending up burnt out and abandoned in the bush or on back streets.

On a Friday evening in mid-November, a well used olive green metallic VZ Commodore was stolen from the driveway of a home in West Tamworth by one of the gang members. Davie was only 16 years of age, but already an experienced car thief. After exchanging the number plates with a similar car from a used car lot in town, the youth knew he had use of the Commodore for at least until Monday before the police were alerted. But he did not anticipate he would not need the car that long.

After picking up two other members – Vince, the gang leader in his mid-thirties and Snow, a blonde-haired, blue-eyed Aboriginal boy in his early teens – Davie took the back roads to Hillvue and on to South Tamworth. He found the laneway that led to the back of the old mechanic's home and to the workshop and drove down slowly. With the laneway blocked at one end, he turned the car around to face the way they had come in, before stopping behind the small cottage.

'Is ziss it?' asked Davie.

'Yeah, I fink so,' replied Vince.

'Who lives 'ere bro?' asked Snow.

'Paulie.'

Neither Davie nor Snow knew who Paulie was, other than he used to be a gang member who had served time in prison. The young teens looked up to Vince as a cross between a father and an older brother. Like Paul, they had come from broken families, as did most of the youths in the gang. But where the others were clearly of Aboriginal descent, with his blonde hair and blue eyes, Snow did not stand out, meaning he was used most often when they planned to rob service stations, convenience stores or take-away outlets.

The arrival of the car outside went unnoticed by the old mechanic and Paul. The pair had already finished dinner; the young Aboriginal was sitting on the lounge watching a police show on television, while the old mechanic was in the laundry putting on a load of washing. The combined noise of the television and the washing machine drowned out any sound made by the car in the laneway outside.

Vince opened his door and left it ajar. 'Youse stay 'ere. Keep it runnin'.'

Davie did not need to be told that he needed to keep the motor running in case they needed to make a quick getaway. He was already on edge due to there being only one way in, and therefore, one way out. They could easily be trapped.

Vince looked around. There was no moon and the only light was from the windows of the small cottage. The night air was cool and still. In the distance a dog barked. He crept slowly to the back door. He could hear the sound of the television above the low rumble of the car at idle. He knocked loudly at the back door and waited.

The old mechanic heard the knock and wondered who could be at the door this late at night. He did not usually get visitors, other than Katie and Mike, but they would always come straight in. Paul did not hear the knock over the sound of the television. The old mechanic switched on the outside light and opened the back door. Vince took a couple of steps backward, and shielded his eyes from the glare of the light bulb.

'Yes, can I help you?'

'We's Paulie?'

The old mechanic took in the scene. On his own, Vince appeared non-threatening, but when seen in company with the two in the car with its motor running, he was not so sure.

'Who wants to know?'

'Vinnie.'

'Hang on a minute.'

The old mechanic closed the door, but left the light on. He went to the lounge room and spoke to Paul.

'There's a bloke at the back door askin' for you.'

'Who is it?'

'Says his name's Vinnie.'

Paul's heart sank. He had been dreading this day. He had hoped that the gang members would forget all about him. But he knew that his past would eventually come calling. Nobody left the gang without there being repercussions. He just hoped that they would listen to reason, but he also knew that Vince was not a reasonable person. Paul was ashen faced as his stood up from the comfortable sofa.

'You don't hafta go if you don't wanna see him. I'll just tell him you're not feelin' well.'

'Nah, it'll be alright.'

He took a deep breath and opened the back door and walked down the ramp until he was a few paces away from Vince.

'Hey bro, whacha doin'?' His false bravado did not fool Vince.

'How come ya di'n't come ta see us, *bro*? How come ya livin' wiff a white fella?'

'He give me a job. I had nowhere else ta stay.'

'But why di'n't ya come ta see us? Ain't we good 'nough for ya no more?'

'Ha! All the time I was inside an' no-one come to see me, not even once. 'Specially after I took the rap for you bastards, *bro*, wasn't *I* good enough for *you*?'

Paul was on the verge of tears, not from fear, but from years of pent up rage. He had never before spoken to Vince in anger. But three and a half years of imprisonment had made him resolute never to run with the gang again, whatever the consequences.

Vince took a few steps backward. He was not used to his minions speaking up for themselves, especially someone low on the pecking order like Paul.

'The pigs mighta picked us up if we come ta see ya in gaol.'

'Yeah, always thinkin' 'bout y'self, hey bro. You jus' didn't give a shit about me. An' now I don't give a shit about you, or the gang.'

'You can't jus' quit bro.'

From his pocket, Vince produced a flick-knife and waved it menacingly at Paul. This time it was he who took a couple of steps backward. The old mechanic, who had been watching proceedings from the safety of the kitchen window, quickly appeared at the door armed with his trusty baseball bat.

'You alright Paul?'

Vince did not immediately see the baseball bat. But when the old mechanic hit the handrail a couple of times, he quickly got the message and backed off.

'Jus' 'cause ya livin' wiff a white fella, don' make *you* a white fella. We'll be waitin' for ya Paulie.'

'You'll be waitin' a long time, bro.'

'You remember Paulie, ya can't jus' quit!'

Vince walked backwards down the path to the waiting car, turned about and hopped inside. From the open window he uttered some obscenities that were drowned out by the roaring engine and the squealing tyres. The old mechanic tried to get the details of the numberplate, but he was too slow.

'Bugger it!'

'What's up?'

'I wasn't quick enough to read the numberplate.'

'Don't worry, they're prob'ly stolen anyway.'

'Who was that guy?'

'Vince, or Vinne, he's the gang leader.'

'He looks like he's led a hard life.'

'Yeah, he's a junk-head. Most o' the cash the gang steals goes ta feedin' his habit.'

'What's a junk-head?'

'Someone who's addicted to ice, you know crystal meth.'

'Oh! Then why don't they just dob him in?' The old mechanic was incredulous.

Paul shrugged his shoulders. 'Fer most of them young fellas, Vinnie's like family. Ya wouldn't dob in your ol' man or ya brother to the cops; they wouldn't dob him in.'

'I think their loyalty's misplaced.'

'I didn't say it was right but.'

Now that Vince knew where Paul was living, he started planning his payback – the sooner the better. He had lost face in front of Davie and Snow, so he had to make sure they were able to see that he was still a strong leader. Like most cowards, he preferred to manipulate situations so others would be placed in the front of more dangerous situations, and this time would be no different. He would get the others to be in the forefront in getting back at Paul and his white fella friend.

Molotov cocktails are simple weapons made using a container filled with a flammable liquid and a burning wick to ignite the liquid. The container of choice is a glass bottle; the flammable liquid, petrol. A wick is often made from a piece of cotton cloth rag stuffed in the mouth of the bottle.

After leaving the laneway at the rear of the old mechanic's cottage, Davie drove to an all-night service station about 10 kilometres to south of Tamworth on the New England Highway. While Vince filled up the car with fuel, Snow and Davie donned balaclavas, made to look like beanies, and entered the station where the unsuspecting operator was serving another customer. The youths took some glass juice bottles from the refrigerator at the rear of the store. When the other customer left, they quickly covered their faces, produced kitchen knives from Davie's backpack and approached the operator, yelling at him to fill the bag with cash and cigarettes.

Vince was waiting in the car with the motor running when the two youths ran from the service station with their bottles and the bag heavy from cash and cigarettes. They had probably been caught on camera, but experience showed that the low resolution of the security cameras was such that the video was mostly useless in identifying individual criminals. Vince gunned the engine even before the two youths had closed their doors. The car fishtailed out onto the highway.

Besides a pair of kitchen knives in his backpack, Davie always came prepared with a plastic tube to be used for siphoning fuel. Sometimes it was needed to put fuel into a car's tank, but at other times, like tonight, it was needed to take fuel out of the tank and into the now empty glass juice bottles.

They did not want to be caught in the dead-end laneway so they parked the car in the side street, about 150 metres from the workshop. After filling the bottles with petrol, they stuffed a piece of cloth they found in the boot into the necks of the bottles. Vince stayed with the car and away from danger. He gave directions to the two youths to light the wicks and toss the petrol bombs at the windows of the workshop. With any luck they would explode inside and wipe out everything in the workshop.

Davie and Snow crept silently down the laneway. Everything was in darkness; even the small cottage they had parked behind just a few hours earlier. The older youth's hands shook with nervous anticipation as he tried to ignite the wick with a cigarette lighter. The plan was to light all three bottles and throw them at the workshop windows all together, but Snow, in his excitement, jumped the gun and threw his bottle first. It exploded on contact and showered burning fuel all down the outside of the wall. Davie quickly ignited the other two bombs and threw them at the other window, before both youths ran for their lives away from the fire.

Both the old mechanic and Paul heard the first explosion. The young Aboriginal jumped out of his bed and peered out of the bedroom window. He saw the fire and witnessed someone throw two more bombs at the workshop window, and the two silhouetted figures running away. He already knew who was involved and why.

The old mechanic ran from his bedroom to the kitchen and looked out of the window. 'Bloody hell, the place's on fire.'

Chapter 14

DO UNTO OTHERS

The old mechanic turned from the kitchen window and went straight to the telephone to ring the emergency number for the fire brigade and the police. He had visions of his entire life's work going up in flames. Feeling a severe bout of anxiety, he needed to sit down. He made his way to the lounge room, sat in his favourite chair and waited. However, his concerns were unfounded because by the time the fire engine turned up, the fire had extinguished itself.

Years ago, after an attempted break-in, the old mechanic had installed wire grates over each of the windows in the workshop. The windows themselves were specially toughened glass that were reinforced with wire. So even though the window panes were cracked by the heat of the burning petrol, they remained more or less intact, limiting the amount of damage inside. The Molotov cocktails merely shattered on the wire grills, spilling their flaming contents on the outside walls. While the exterior wall of the workshop was scorched and blackened by the fire, because the building was constructed of corrugated iron sheeting over a galvanised steel frame, the interior of the workshop suffered almost no damage. The fire was spectacular, but the damage was minimal.

When Paul saw what had happened, he raced to the kitchen, out the back door and after the fleeing youths. He was gaining on them, but they made it to the stolen vehicle before he could catch them.

In his frustration and fury, he yelled at the fleeing vehicle, 'Ahhh! I'm gonna get you bastards!'

Paul was breathing heavily as he turned around and walked back to the workshop. Like the old mechanic, he feared that everything he had worked for had been burnt in the fire. So, he was surprised and elated to find that the fire had just about burnt itself out.

In the distance he heard the siren of the fire truck, so he waited at the end of the laneway to show the way to where the fire had been burning just minutes previously. There was a strong smell of petrol in the cool air, and the scorch marks of the fire were evident in the headlights of the fire truck. Glass from the smashed bottles crunched underfoot as the fire chief examined the area. Eventually he turned to the young Aboriginal mechanic.

'Who are you?' asked the fire chief.

'Paul, I live 'ere.'

'Did you see who did it?'

Paul was initially unsure how to answer. Even though he knew who was behind the fire, and the reason the workshop was targeted, he actually did not see the faces of the two youths who threw the petrol bombs, and nor did he know their names.

'I seen a coupla kids runnin' away. I don' know who they are but.'

The truth would eventually come out, but now was not the time.

It suddenly dawned on Paul that the old mechanic was nowhere to be seen. He ran back into the house. The only light was on in the kitchen, but he was not there.

'George, where are ya?'

'In the lounge room,' the old mechanic croaked.

Paul went through into the lounge room, switching on the light as he entered. He found the old mechanic sitting in his chair, a look of despair on his face. His breathing was laboured. He did not look well.

'You awright?'

'Is there anything left?'

'Yeah, … everything!'

Paul smiled.

'Wha' d'ya mean?'

'The fire went out itself. Come an' see.'

Paul helped the old mechanic out of the chair and followed him outside to where the fire chief was speaking to a couple of police officers. One of the police officers, a senior constable, turned to the old mechanic as he approached. Paul kept his distance.

'Are you the proprietor of this establishment?'

'Yeah, I suppose. I own it with my son-in-law and daughter.'

'Do you know who might've done this?'

'I've got an idea.'

'Tell me.'

The old mechanic turned around to Paul before he continued, and motioned for the young Aboriginal to join him.

'We had a visitor earlier this evening. A guy by the name of Vince, an acquaintance of my friend here. He made a number of threats to Paul.'

The senior constable turned to Paul. 'What relation is this person Vince to you?'

'He ain't nothin' to me now. He's the leader of a gang I used ta be in.'

'So, was it Vince who threw the petrol bombs at this building?' asked the senior constable, pointing at the workshop.

'No.'

He gave a puzzled look. 'Then who threw the petrol bombs?'

'Vince always gets others ta do his dirty work.'

'So, did you see who *did* throw the petrol bombs?'

'I seen 'em runnin' away. I didn't get a good look at their faces but. I chased 'em up the lane; they got away but.'

'How did they make their escape?'

'In a dark coloured Commodore.'

'Could you identify them if you saw them again?'

'I dunno, prob'ly not. One of 'em had blonde hair but.'

'So why do you think this Vince person wanted to set fire to this building?'

'As payback. He wasn't real happy I didn't wanna join his gang again.'

'When were you last in his gang?'

Paul was getting uncomfortable with the line of questioning. He did not want to admit to the police officer that he was an ex-convict, but it seemed inevitable that the truth would eventually come out.

In a low voice he said, 'Before I went inside.'

At first the senior constable did not realise what Paul meant. But then it registered.

'What were you inside for?'

The old mechanic interrupted the questioning. 'Does it matter? Paul's not on trial here, but the one who did this should be. If you wanna make us all safe again, go and find the bastard behind this and other crimes in Tamworth.'

Suitably chastened, the senior constable asked, 'Does Vince have a second name?'

Paul had only ever known Vince by his first name. If he did have a surname, Paul did not know it. 'We only ever called him Vince or Vinnie.'

The senior constable already knew who Vince was. The police had been trying for years to obtain enough evidence to convict him and break up his gang, but he had always slipped through their fingers. He expected that this time would be no different.

The Golden Rule states: "Do unto others as you would have them do unto you." It is a rule that is widely known through many cultures and belief systems that you should treat others the same way that you would want them to treat you. But there is another rule that some people follow: "Do unto others, *before* they can do unto you". It is a rule about striking first and the rule that many gang members follow. It is also the rule that Paul was most familiar with.

Vince had already made the first move. It was only through misfortune that he missed getting back at Paul. Next time fortune might be on the gang leader's side. Paul had to make sure there would not be a next time. But he could not do anything on his own; he needed help.

Uncle Danny Stewart was no friend of Vince or his gang. For a number of years, the gang leader's activities had been having a negative impact on the wider Aboriginal and Torres Strait Islander Community in Tamworth and the string of offences attributed to the gang had brought much disharmony within the community and soured its otherwise good relations with the police.

After being contacted by Paul and briefed on the events of the previous evening, Uncle Danny quickly arranged to have a meeting with the Local Area Command's Police Aboriginal Liaison Officer (PALO) and Paul. The meeting would be in the Kamilaroi Community Centre in West Tamworth on Saturday afternoon. Uncle Danny collected Paul on the way, as he thought the motorcycle might attract unwanted attention.

When Paul entered the room, he was taken aback when he saw that the senior constable from the previous night was seated at the table. Uncle Danny introduced Paul to the PALO, who in turn introduced both Aboriginals to the senior constable, who was now dressed in civilian clothing.

'What's he doin' here?' asked Paul, a concerned look on his face.

'Don't be afraid of me son, I want to put Vincent Rogers behind bars as much as anyone. We've been chasing him for years, but we've only been able to catch the minnows, like yourself.'

'I ain't afraid of you, but I am afraid of Vinnie. I know what he c'n do.'

'Well, hopefully he won't be doin' it for much longer,' said the PALO.

'The way I see it,' said Uncle Danny, 'you can't catch someone if you doesn't know where 'e is.'

Everyone nodded in agreement.

'My people tells me 'e couch-surfs most nights. 'E don't sleep more 'n two nights in any one place.'

'That's one of the problems we have,' advised the senior constable.

'They also tell me 'e's been seein' a sheila in North Tamworth. I think she supplies 'im with the drugs 'e takes. If she doesn't, then she knows where ta gedit.'

'That's fine, but using ice is just a misdemeanour. If he gets to court, the magistrate will prob'ly just give him a slap on the wrist, and he'll be straight out to create mischief and mayhem again. Finding the guy is one thing, finding evidence for a serious offence that stands up in court is another thing completely.'

'What kind of evidence?' asked Paul.

The senior constable looked long at the young Aboriginal mechanic before speaking. 'Umm, well, material evidence like catching him in possession of the proceeds of crime. Umm, or there's eye witness accounts, preferably corroborated, but it'd have to be for serious crimes like assault or something like that.'

'What about conspiracy to commit a crime?'

'Like what?'

'Armed robbery, BE&S, assault occasioning actual bod'ly harm, arson, car theft, criminal damage.'

'You have evidence that Rogers was involved in all that?' the senior constable was shocked.

'Vinnie was the master-mind behind all that stuff; he just got others to do it for 'im.'

'But you have proof?'

'I know someone inside; he got screwed by Vinnie, just like me. If he's prepared to back me up, I'll give ya a statement.'

'It could be dangerous,' cautioned Uncle Danny. 'If word gets out that ya dobbed 'im in, people might think ya done wrong.'

'Uncle Danny, Vinnie won't stop 'til he gets me back in the gang, or hurts me or my friends. The only thing that'll stop him is if he ends up in goal or he gets killed. If I had my way, I'd rather see him taken out, but the cops might not be happy with that. Gaol's the next best.'

Paul gave the details of the prison inmate – Daryl Porter – to the senior constable. Arrangements were made for Uncle Danny to go to the prison first and speak with him. If Daryl was prepared to give evidence, the police would get statements from him and Paul. They would then get the local Magistrate to issue warrants for the gang leader's arrest before letting the justice system take over.

The only problem with the plan that Paul could see was, how would he, the old mechanic, Michael, Katie and baby Kieran keep safe until Vincent Rogers was put behind bars. On the way home he made his concerns known to Uncle Danny.

'Why don' cha come an' stay with me fer a bit, until Vinnie's not a problem no more?'

'Are ya sure? I don' wanna be a nuisance.'

Uncle Danny smiled at his young friend. 'You're a good nuisance Paulie. An' we don' want them nice white fellas gittin' 'urt now, do we?'

'No, that's for sure.'

Now that Vince knew where Paul lived and worked, everyone associated with him was in potential danger.

On the following Monday, Uncle Danny visited Tamworth Correctional Centre. While it was made to seem just part of his normal routine, he actually came to see Paul's friend and former gang member, Daryl Porter. Although he was initially reluctant to help for fear of retribution, when it was made clear that his evidence would be given in secret and that Paul would likewise make a statement, he agreed.

Within a week, the local magistrate had issued warrants for the arrest of Vincent Rogers, and five days later he was arrested after the stolen car he was driving failed to stop at a Police RBT/RDT. After a short chase, he crashed the car and was arrested, together with Davie, Snow and one other youth named Joey. A search of the car revealed a handgun hidden in the glove compartment.

Due to the seriousness of the charges against him, being of no fixed abode and thus deemed a flight risk, Vince was remanded in custody until he was committed for trial. Bail was applied for but formally denied. At his trial, he was found guilty of all charges and sentenced to ten years imprisonment, of which seven years were to be without parole, to be served at Long Bay Correctional Centre in Sydney. Davie and Joey were convicted on several charges and were each sentenced to six months detention in a Juvenile Detention Facility. Snow was cautioned and given a good behaviour bond.

    With Vince in prison in Sydney, and several other members in gaol in Tamworth, there was no-one left to lead the gang. The junior members drifted back into their community.

BE&S – break, enter and steal
RBT – random breath testing
RDT – random drug testing

Chapter 15

SAVING GRACE

When news of the arson attack was broadcast on the local radio on Saturday morning, Michael and Katie were alarmed. A quick phone call allayed their fears, but nevertheless they drove around to survey the damage for themselves, and to comfort the still shaken old mechanic. Paul had wanted to sweep up the glass from the broken bottles, but the Police Forensic Team had yet to examine the scene to check the fragments for any finger prints. He had already made arrangements to meet with Uncle Danny. While he waited for the Elder to pick him up, he was helping with the housework.

The petrol fumes had dissipated by the time Michael and Katie arrived, but the blackened scars on the exterior walls were still clearly evident. In time the corrugated iron sheets would need to be replaced due to the zinc coating being damaged by the heat; the panels would eventually rust. They hoped that the business' insurance policy would cover the cost of replacing the cracked window glass and the fire affected iron sheets in the event of an arson attack.

After opening the workshop doors, and examining the interior of the workshop, Michael quickly realised how fortunate they had been. The saving grace was that there was nothing flammable on the inside of the walls below the windows that had been attacked. A mere trickle of burning petrol had seeped through the cracked glass and run down the inside of the wall, but with nothing else to catch alight the fire extinguished itself. However, if the petrol bombs had been thrown at the windows on the opposite wall, even though they were similarly protected, the bare timber frames of Katie's office and the storeroom directly below the windows could easily have caught fire, which would likely have spread to the rest of the workshop.

After locking up, Michael joined the rest of the family inside the cottage.

'Have you any idea who did it?' he asked.

'Oh, we know who was responsible,' replied the old mechanic, 'we just can't prove it.'

'Who?' asked Katie.

'The leader of the gang that Paul use ta belong to.'

'How do you know it was him? Did ya see him do it?' asked Michael.

'He came 'round earlier last night and made some threats to Paul.'

'But if you know it was him, why can't the police arrest him?' asked Katie.

'Because we didn't actually see him throw the petrol bombs.'

Paul entered the room and joined in the conversation. 'He always gets the younger ones in the gang to do 'is dirty work. He's like a puppeteer, pullin' the strings. Ya know he's in control; ya can't prove it but. If the young ones get caught, he just cuts the strings.'

'You know, we were so lucky,' said Michael. 'If they'd thrown the petrol bombs at the back windows instead of the front ones, we could've lost everything. And I mean everything: tools, spares, service manuals, all the workbenches, furnishings, computer records, the truck, your Dommie and Kieran's Bonnie – the whole lot could've been destroyed.'

'Not to mention any customer bikes that hadn't been collected,' added the old mechanic.

'We'd better check our insurance is up-to-date,' suggested Katie. 'I wouldn't be surprised if we're actually under-insured. Now's a good time we updated everything.'

'What're we gonna do if that thug comes back?' posed Michael.

'Hopefully the cops'll be able to do somethin',' replied the old mechanic, although he was not completely confident.

'I'm gonna see Uncle Danny th's arvo,' said Paul. 'He said he might be able to help.'

'But what can he do?' asked Katie.

Paul shrugged his shoulders. He felt terrible that he had placed his work friends in danger. He did not know what Uncle Danny would be able to do, but the Kamilaroi Elder was his only hope.

When Paul returned home from his meeting with Uncle Danny, the PALO and the senior constable, he was in a much brighter mood. The old mechanic was in the kitchen folding the dry laundry items he had retrieved from the clothes line. His wife and Katie would have ironed about half the items, but he hated ironing, and only did what was absolutely necessary. None of the items in his basket fitted into that category.

'How'd the meeting with Uncle Danny go?' asked the old mechanic.

'Great! He invited the Aboriginal Liaison Officer, and the cop from last night was there too.'

Paul explained what was discussed and how they planned to deal with Vince and his gang.

'But won't that put you in even greater danger?' suggested the old mechanic, a concerned look on his face.

'I don't reck'n I could be in any more danger than I already am. As I said to 'em at the meetin', Vinnie won't stop 'til I'm back in the gang or someone knocks 'im off. I'd rather see 'im dead, but I might be in trouble with the cops if that happens. I can't see how else we can stop 'im.'

'But what're you gonna do between now and when he gets arrested? You're still on his "most wanted" list.'

'Uncle Danny said I could go an' stay with 'im. I'd still come in ta work each day – Vinnie's too gutless ta try anythin' durin' daytime hours. If 'e comes 'round after dark, tell 'im I don't live 'ere no more.'

The old mechanic almost voiced his further concerns. That is all well and good, but what if he does not knock next time? What if he just sends more petrol bombs our way? But he kept his concerns to himself. He just hoped that fortune would be on their side yet again.

Paul packed all the clothes he would need, as well as his toiletries into his backpack. He moved his work clothes to the change room inside the workshop, and wheeled his Triumph out into the laneway. After starting the engine, and leaving it on the centre-stand to warm up, he went back inside to say goodbye to the old mechanic.

'I'm goin' now. Will you be awright?'

'Yeah, I'll be fine. See ya Mond'y.'

'You looked a bit crook when I seen ya in the lounge room las' night.'

'Yeah, I just got a bit of a fright, that's all. Don't you worry about me, I'll be okay.'

He scrawled a number on a scrap of paper and gave it to the old mechanic. 'Here's Uncle Danny's number – if ya need me, give him a call, I'll come straight 'round.'

The old mechanic thought that if he needed someone urgently, he would call the emergency number – 000 – but he took the Kamilaroi Elder's number anyway.

'Looks like I'll hafta start cookin' for meself again.'

'If everythin' goes ta plan, I'll be back in a week.'

'And if it doesn't?'

Paul smiled, but left the question hanging. He did not want to think about what might happen if the plan did not work.

Besides providing shelter and protection for Paul, Uncle Danny had another reason for offering accommodation to the young Aboriginal. While still an inmate at Tamworth Correctional Centre, Paul had stood out as polite toward others and respectful of his culture. He was impressed that Paul had persevered in completing his motorcycle mechanics apprenticeship when so many others dropped out, and pleased that he had been able to secure employment. That he also found accommodation with his employer afforded further recognition – many Aboriginal youths would not live with anyone but members of their own family. The fact that he had a criminal record was neither here nor there for Uncle Danny, nobody was perfect. He was more concerned with the future than the past.

Uncle Danny's daughter and son-in-law were concerned that their only daughter, Grace, had not been particularly successful in love. While there were not a large number of eligible young men in their church, they felt that she was becoming too selective. Even though she was only in her early twenties, they were starting to feel that she might never get married, let alone bear a grandchild for them. They had met Paul at the barbecue several weeks earlier, but they were concerned that he did not go to church. Not being a church-goer himself, Uncle Danny held no such misgivings, so he invited his granddaughter to have dinner with them that Saturday night.

Dressed for dinner, rather than a barbecue, Grace paid a bit more attention to her appearance, especially when she found out that Paul would also be there. Gone were the jeans and t-shirt, and in their place a white floral dress. Her dark wavy hair was allowed to flow over her shoulders, and she had light makeup on her face. She was in effect dressed to impress.

No longer "ordinary looking", Paul could hardly keep his eyes off her when she entered the dining room behind her grandmother, carrying the platter laden with their roast dinner. Grace, for her part was demure, and kept her eyes lowered, even when she spoke, which was not very often. While her appearance had changed, her personality was still the same polite sweetness.

Paul found her much more attractive than he had at the barbecue. Clearly besotted, he could not later recall what was discussed over dinner. Before he realised, the main course was over and the table was being cleared. In Uncle Danny's house, the kitchen was the domain of the women. If men entered the room, they were encouraged to pass through quickly and not to linger, indeed, Aunty Dot insisted on it. Men were allowed to cook, but only on the barbecue in the backyard. Otherwise, cooking was "women's secret business."

When the two women left the room, Paul said, 'You didn't tell me Grace'd be havin' dinner with us too.'

'I didn't think I 'ad ta,' replied Uncle Danny with a smile. 'She's nice ain't she?'

Paul blushed. 'I don't think she'd be int'rested in me but.'

'Why not?'

'She goes ta church, an' I'm an ex-con.'

'You changed Paulie. You're not the same boy you was when ya went to gaol. Yeah, you're an ex-con, but th' import'nt part is "ex". Ya don't think I'd trust ya with Gracie if I thought you was still runnin' wild with that gang, do ya?'

'No. She goes to church but.'

'So! If ya worried 'bout that, start goin' yaself. Ya might like it. It's a black fella church. I know the folks who go; they're nice people.'

'Yeah, but ya hafta be a good person ta go there, and I ain't. I been ta prison.'

Uncle Danny smiled. 'If ya had ta be good ta go ta church, no-one'd be let in the front door. Church ain't for good people, but it's fer people who wanna be good. Don' you wanna be good?'

'Yeah, but ...'

Paul was going to ask why Uncle Danny did not go to church himself, but thought better of it. He did not want to be thought disrespectful.

Other than the chapel at his mother's funeral, the young Aboriginal mechanic's only experience of church was as a young child when his oldest sister took him to the local Roman Catholic Church. He still remembered being touched inappropriately by the parish priest. He was confused and never told anybody, but thankfully never went back to that church, or indeed any church. He wondered if Grace's church would be any different.

Paul's thoughts were interrupted when the two women returned to the dining room bearing two bowls each of dessert. As Grace passed one of the bowls to Paul, their hands touched briefly. She blushed and lowered her head, averting her eyes.

Automatically she said 'Sorry.'

'What for?'

Slowly she raised her head until their eyes met. Paul was smiling. She blushed again, but this time she kept her head and eyes up. They sat back down around the dining table and began to eat dessert – apple crumble and ice-cream.

Halfway through Paul said, 'Tell me 'bout ya church.'

Grace looked up excitedly. 'D'ya wanna come?'

'Maybe.'

'Well, there's lotsa music an' singin'; people clappin' hands an' everyone's real friendly.'

'Do they have priests?'

'Nah. We gotta minister but, he's pretty cool. He reads the Bible an' prays 'n stuff. An' when the service's over, we have lotsa real nice food, an' somethin' to drink.'

'Doesn't sound like anythin' I remember.'

'Me too,' added Uncle Danny.

'What time's it start?'

'Ten o'clock, but some come early, and some come late. If ya get there before ten ya get to choose where ya sit but. If ya come late, ya hafta take what's left.'

'D'ya hafta get all dressed up? I don't have any good clobber.'

'Nah, it's pretty relaxed. Wear wha'cha got on now.'

Paul was wearing jeans and a short-sleeved polo shirt.

'Is it awright if I ride me bike?'

'Yeah, but we c'n pick ya up on the way, if ya like.'

'Okay, what time?'

'9:30.'

'Shouldn't ya check with ya mum firs',' suggested Uncle Danny.

'Nah, she'll be right.'

The Aboriginal Church of Christ service was so very unlike anything that Paul had ever before experienced. The people were very welcoming and friendly towards him. He recognised a number of them whom he had seen in different circumstances, including at his mother's funeral, but no-one made him feel uncomfortable, or suggested that he was not good enough to be there. He enjoyed the singing, and especially the small band playing country and western style tunes to many of the traditional hymns and songs. But most of all, he enjoyed sitting with Grace.

After the service, Grace introduced Paul to the minister.

'Ah Paul. Yes, I've heard about you.'

Paul's heart sank.

'You're a motorcycle mechanic, aren't you?'

Chapter 16

LIVING ON THE EDGE

Just like the old mechanic had initially feared, Vince Rogers and his cohorts thought that they had been successful in destroying the workshop with their petrol bombs. And not being able to read nor interested in watching or hearing the news, they had not heard that the firebombs had been spectacularly unsuccessful in devastating the building and the livelihood of Paul and his friends. By the time they did hear, they were already in custody, and so unable to do anything about it.

Unfortunately, neither Paul, nor his workmates knew that Vince and his gang were ignorant of the fact that the arson attack had not destroyed the workshop. So, they continued living on the edge of uncertainty, waiting for the gang to return. The old mechanic was the one who suffered the most insecurity. He slept very uneasily after Paul moved out and was awoken by every tiny sound during the night. Even during the day, he was unnerved by every car entering the laneway or driving past. By Tuesday morning, he was a nervous wreck.

The four workers gathered for their early morning cuppa. The two younger mechanics were talking about riding their bikes, while the old mechanic was staring off into space. Katie made her own tea before sitting down in the spare chair. After taking a sip she looked over at her father. He looked tired and drawn.

'Are you alright Dad?' she asked, a concerned look on her face.

The old mechanic did not respond. The other two stopped talking and turned their attention to the old mechanic.

'Dad!'

He was startled and nearly spilled his mug of tea.

Katie repeated her question. 'Are you alright? You look really tired.'

He looked around the circle of anxious faces, suddenly embarrassed and shook his head.

'No, not really. I'm just so buggered. I've hardly slept a wink since Frid'y night when those bastards came callin'. I'm jus' gettin' too old for all this crap. Sorry sweetheart.'

'Do you want one of us to come and stay with you?'

'Nah, what's the point. Mike's the only one available, and he's got you an' the bub to worry about. No, I'll be awright, I jus' need a decent sleep.'

'We can manage here today if you wanna go get some shut-eye now,' said Michael. 'Me an' Paul can handle everything between us.'

'Are you sure?'

'Of course.'

The old mechanic did not need much convincing. He finished his tea and tottered off out of the workshop toward home. Paul, who had not said anything, followed him out.

'George.'

The old mechanic stopped and turned around. He looked as old and weary as he felt.

'I'm sorry.'

'What about?'

'Fer gettin' you inta this mess.'

Paul seemed to be on the verge of tears. Despite his great weariness, the old mechanic suddenly felt great compassion for the young Aboriginal, and placed a hand on his shoulder. He wanted to say something profound, but could not think what; he was just too tired.

'I'll be awright Paul. Go an' help Mike and Katie.'

The old mechanic slept soundly for most of the day, only waking to a soft knocking at his bedroom door. He looked at the clock on his bedside table, showing that it was 3:50.

Katie opened the door. 'Are you awake?'

He yawned. 'Yeah, thanks sweetheart.'

'Did you sleep?'

'Like a baby.'

'That's good. Mike and I want you to come around to our place for dinner later on.'

'Thanks sweetheart, but I'll be awright. Besides, those bastards might come back tonight.'

'So, what if they do. You couldn't stop them anyway; not on your own.'

'You might be right. But I'm not gonna go out and enjoy myself while some drugged-up, low-life, scum-bag, gangster does his level best at destroying everything I've worked for these past 55 years. I'm jus' not gonna do it.'

Katie could sometimes be just as stubborn as her father.

'Very well, if Mohammad won't come to the mountain, the mountain will come to Mohammad. We'll be having dinner with you then. See you at a quarter to six.'

With that, she turned on her heels and left the house. The subject would not tolerate further discussion.

Since she had commenced working full time again, Katie had been juggling work with the responsibilities of being a mother and a wife. To allow her to do what she was best qualified at – cook meals and breast-feed baby Kieran – Michael now did many of the more menial tasks around the house, like setting and clearing the table, washing up, cleaning and vacuuming the unit and washing their clothes. Other tasks, like playing with the baby and changing his nappies, were usually shared.

Nevertheless, because of a lack of time and general tiredness at the end of the day, meals were often prepared in advance and frozen, or else soups and stews were prepared in a crock pot and allowed to cook through the day, ready for dinner that night. When the family returned home, they would be greeted by the delicious aromas of the meal-of-the-day. All they needed to do was dish it up and eat. But on this particular night, they merely packed up the crock pot containing an Irish Stew and returned to the old mechanic's cottage, right on 5:45.

He greeted his daughter with a kiss. Taking his grandson from her arms, he directed Michael to place the crock pot on the kitchen bench. Even though the lid was still in place, he could smell the mouth-watering aromas wafting around his small kitchen.

'When did ya cook this?'

'Today,' replied Katie.

He frowned. 'But you were at work today.'

Katie smiled. 'Yeah, but I'm a woman Dad.'

'Wonder Woman more like it.'

'It's a crock pot George,' said Michael. 'We just turn it on in the morning, and when we get home it's already cooked.'

'Spoil sport,' replied Katie.

'Don't worry Sweetheart, you're *my* Wonder Woman,' declared the old mechanic.

'Thanks Dad.'

'Ah, flattery will get you nowhere,' said Michael.

In response, Katie gave her father a cuddle and a kiss on the cheek.

'Who says?' replied the old mechanic.

'Well, it doesn't get me anywhere.' Michael dropped his lower lip in a mock sulk.

Katie turned to Michael with her arms out. 'Oh, poor Mikey, always left out, come and get a kiss and a cuddle.'

While receiving a peck on the cheek and a hug from his wife, he noticed over her shoulder a car driving slowly down the laneway.

'There's a car outside,' he warned.

The old mechanic jumped up, baby Kieran still in his arms, and peered through the window. 'I don't think they're from the gang.'

'Stay here; I'll just go an' see who it is,' advised Michael.

He quickly left through the back door, leaving Katie and his father-in-law huddled at the kitchen window. It was still light enough to see. The unmarked police car had already turned around and was coming slowly back toward Michael. The front seat passenger opened his window.

'Who are you?' asked Michael.

The front seat passenger showed Michael his identification. 'Senior Constable Robison and Constable Tyler. And you are?'

'Mike Jones, I work here and my father-in-law lives here. What're you doing?'

'This's now part of our patrol. Until Vince Rogers is behind bars and his gang's broken up, we're keeping a watching brief on these premises.'

'Thank goodness, my father-in-law'll be happy. How often are you gonna come by?'

'As often as needed.'

'Thanks, I'll let him know. He might be able to sleep now.'

The old mechanic was not the only one having trouble sleeping. Paul was not just concerned about whether he was doing the right thing by providing the police with enough evidence to put Vince Rogers behind bars for a long time. He was also worried about how his actions would be perceived by the local Aboriginal and Torres Strait Islander Community.

Despite the best efforts of the Police Local Area Commander and the Police Aboriginal Liaison Officers, the police were seen by some in the community as the enemy. Just as in any organisation, there were some members of the NSW Police Force who were overtly racist. The actions of some were often seen as indicative of the organisation as a whole. Thus, any assistance provided to the police to catch those members of the community who had committed criminal acts was often seen as a betrayal of their race. He put his concerns to Uncle Danny.

Despite his initial misgivings, the Kamilaroi Elder smiled. 'If you done wrong Paulie, then I must'a done even more wrong. There's a old sayin': the dingo don't shit in 'is own den. But that fella Vince, he shit in white fellas' dens *and* black fellas' dens. He don't care where he shit. There's a lotta bad blood in our mob 'cos of what he done, gittin' the youngens ta commit crimes and makin' 'em take the blame, landin' 'em in gaol. If someone says you done wrong, tell 'em to come an' see me.'

'Thanks Uncle Danny.'

'Now, how you an' Gracie doin'? You want me to talk to her mumma?'

Paul was suddenly embarrassed. 'Grace is real nice, but I don' wanna rush things.'

'Do ya like 'er?'

'Of course I like her, she's a nice girl.'

'Well, wha d'ya waitin' for?'

'I'm not sure she likes me as much.'

'Ah Paulie, Aunty Dot tells me she don' jus' like you, she love you. She can't stop talkin' 'bou'cha. So, talk to 'er, tell 'er how yer feelin'.'

'And then what?'

'Then youse c'n git married, o' course.'

'But I'm not sure I'm ready for marriage Uncle Danny.'

'Ah Paulie. Ya got a girl, ya got a job, an' ya got someplace ta live; of course ya're ready.'

Life seemed so simple from Uncle Danny's perspective. But having come from a broken home, where violence and abuse were more common than love and care, Paul had misgivings about forming a permanent relationship with someone, especially someone he had only recently met. He did not even know how he would respond to being in a domestic relationship, let alone how living with Grace would be. He needed time.

'I'm sorry Uncle Danny, but I ain't ready ta make that commitment jus' yet. I like Grace, I like her a lot. I ain't ready fer marriage but.'

Rather than be angry or upset, Uncle Danny was even more impressed with the maturity shown by the young Aboriginal.

'Ya know Paulie, I think ya're ready to make that commitment. But *you* gotta be comf'table with that decision, *you* gotta know in yaself. But don' take too long d'cidin', Gracie might not wait.'

'That's the risk I'm prepared ta take, Uncle Danny.'

Unknown to Paul, Grace had been having a similar conversation with her mother. She told her mother that she loved Paul and was even prepared to live with him if it meant that they could be together. Of course, being Christians, living together out of wedlock was not on the cards. However,

Grace said she was prepared to leave the church if that was the case. Where the conversation between the two men ended on friendly terms, that between mother and daughter ended in tears.

The following morning, instead of going to work, Grace waited around the corner for her parents to leave the house. She had already packed some clothes and some things she thought she would need and left the bag under her bed. She went back inside and wrote a note. From her bedroom she took the bag, changed into her jeans and left the house again. A bus took her into town and another out to South Tamworth.

Grace wandered around the streets, looking for the workshop where Paul worked. She knew the general area, but not the precise location. At last she entered a sandwich shop and asked for help. Jessie, the shop assistant, pointed her in the right direction.

By the time she entered the laneway, the bag was getting so heavy she needed a rest. Michael was just about to take a customer's BSA for a test run when he spied a young Aboriginal woman at the end of the lane. He returned to the workshop and called to his workmate.

'Hey Paul, I think you've got a visitor.'

Chapter 17

NEW ARRANGEMENTS

Paul had mixed emotions at seeing Grace. While he was delighted that she had shown such trust in him and their relationship, and that her actions had demonstrated her feelings for him, he was still concerned that her parents would strenuously object to their relationship, let alone her taking up residence with him. Despite what Uncle Danny had said, he still felt he needed to take his time before making a firm commitment, and that included cohabiting. Grace turning up at the workshop added a further level of complication to the situation, particularly as Paul was now living temporarily at her grandparent's place.

The most appropriate solution would be for Grace to take up residence with Uncle Danny and Aunty Dot and for Paul to move back to live with the old mechanic. But with the uncertainty surrounding the capture and arrest of Vince and his gang, this did not seem such a wise choice. A decision had to be made, and quickly. During the mid-morning smoko break, the young Aboriginal called the Kamilaroi Elder.

After speaking with Uncle Danny, Paul felt somewhat relieved. He joined the small group having morning tea.

'Wha' did he say?' asked Michael.

'He said he's got plenty of room at his place and that Grace was welcome to stay there too. He's comin' 'round after lunch to pick her up.'

Katie looked across to Grace who appeared to be somewhat disappointed with the new arrangement. 'Are you happy with that Grace?' she asked.

'I wanted to move in with Paulie.'

Paul was a bit embarrassed by her public announcement that she wanted to live with him.

Michael came to his rescue. 'Actually, you *are* going to be living together, or at least living under the same roof. You'll just be chaperoned for a time. Then, once this gang problem's resolved, you can choose what you wanna do.'

The new arrangement was well pleasing to Paul, as it allowed him more time to get to know Grace, without the pressure of being in a relationship. To him, it was the best solution. And it was another reason why he had so much love and respect for Uncle Danny. He just hoped that Grace's parents were agreeable with her staying with her grandparents under their supervision. As it turned out, they had little choice.

As they were speaking, a car drove down the laneway and parked outside the workshop. Michael went outside to greet their visitor – it was Paul's Parole Officer, Bob Petersen.

'G'day Bob. You come to check up on Paul.'

'Yeah, I heard you've had a few dramas here. Is everything alright?'

Michael outlined the events of the previous weekend before calling for Paul. The Aboriginal mechanic then explained that he was now living temporarily with the Kamilaroi Elder, Uncle Danny Stewart, until Vince Rogers and his gang were no longer a threat. Once the Parole Officer was satisfied with the new living arrangements, he left, although he did wonder why the alternate accommodation had not been an option when Paul was first released from prison.

Katie had a number of her friends on Facebook. Since she had left her office job, it was the best way of keeping in touch with her friends and former work colleagues. Rather than having to check each individual friend's page, she would instead receive an e-mail whenever the page owner posted a message to Facebook.

Later that evening, before she retired to bed, Katie received a message that Lilly had at last posted something to Facebook. She read the post before she turned out the light.

'Are you awake Mikey?' she asked quietly.

There was no reply.

It was not until the quartet sat down for their first cup of the day the next morning that Katie had a chance to tell the others of the Facebook post from Lilly.

'There's good news, and not so good news,' she announced.

Everyone looked to her expectantly.

'Lilly has finally posted something to Facebook.'

'That's great,' said Michael, 'wha' did she say?'

'She wrote a poem called *Despair*; it's pretty sad.' Katie then read the poem out loud.

An incredible heaviness drags me down;
I scarce can lift my head to see
The blue skies, or the happy child
Who's playing by her mother's knee.

There is no joy, no happiness
To elevate my sullen mood.
And all about me keep away,
So I just sit alone and brood.

There was a time when I'd delight
In light and life and different hues.

But light has dimmed and colour drained
And life is now a cruel ruse.

How came about this great despair,
That I should live my days in grief?
'Twas loss of one I held so dear,
His life since taken by a thief.

    No-one said anything for a few long minutes.
    At last the old mechanic voiced the views of everyone. 'That's so sad.'
    There was more silence. Katie had tears in her eyes.
    He spoke again. 'Everyone deals with grief differently. Some people like to talk about how they feel. Some people don't believe they can speak the unspeakable, and so they write about how they feel. I think it's good that Lilly's able to write. As sad as that poem is, I think it's a step in the right direction on her road to healin' and recovery. And the fact she's posted that to Facebook suggests she wants to reengage with her friends.'
    'Did you "Like" the post?' asked Michael.
    'Yeah, but I felt funny doing so. How do you "Like" something so sad and poignant?'
    Another poem appeared on Lilly's Facebook page over the weekend. Katie advised the others on the following Monday morning.
    'This one's called *The Land of Silence* and I think it's just as sad as the first one.' Katie then read the second poem out loud.

There is no-one to hear in the Land of Silence;
No-one speaks, and there is none who listens.
Cries go unanswered.
There is no-one to see in the Land of Silence;

There is neither light, nor darkness.
There is no sun, no moon, and no stars.
There is no knowledge in the Land of Silence;
No wisdom, no learning, and no experiences.
There is no-one who thinks,
And no-one who remembers.
There is no-one who feels in the Land of Silence;
No-one cares, and no-one to show empathy.
There is no love, no compassion,
No happiness or joy;
Emotions have died.
There is no faith, and no hope.
There is nothing to give warmth,
And nothing to cool.
There is no wind, no rain,
No hail and no snow.
There is no water in the Land of Silence;
Nothing grows:
No trees, no grass, and no plants.
No oceans, no seas,
No rivers and no lakes.
There are no beasts of the field,
No birds of the air,
No fishes of the seas,
No creatures great or small.
There is no sustenance in the Land of Silence;
There is nothing to sate the appetite,
Or quench the thirst.
There is no life, and neither is there death;
There is no beginning and no ending.
There is only existence.

Just as after the first poem, there was a period of silence when Katie had finished reading.

Eventually Michael asked, 'What do you think she means by the Land of Silence? Is that where she thinks she is?'

No-one replied immediately.

At last Katie suggested, 'It sounds like she's saying that she's existing in the Land of Silence.'

Paul commented, 'In Aboriginal culture, the Land of Silence or the Land of Eternal Dreamin' is the place spirits go to when a person dies.'

'I think you'll find that's the case in a number of other cultures as well Paul,' advised the old mechanic. 'In Jewish culture, Sheol, or the place of the dead is also called the Land of Silence.'

'Is that the same as Limbo and Purgatory?' asked Michael.

'I think there're a whole host of different terms — Abaddon, Hades and Gehenna come to mind — that different cultures and belief systems use to describe the same place,' informed the old mechanic.

'I don't care what it's called or where it is,' said Katie, 'it doesn't sound like a very inviting place to visit … or even exist.'

'You sure wouldn't go there for ya holid'ys but,' added Paul.

The mood in the workshop was somewhat subdued and sullen following the reading of the poem and subsequent discussion.

'I think it's time we got to work,' advised Michael, 'or our customers'll be thinking we're all working in the Land of Silence.'

Everyone laughed, appreciating the flippant remark to lighten the mood.

As Paul's competence improved, along with his experience, so the more he was able to do, thereby lightening the work load on the others. So, despite late November being the busiest season for motorcycle riding, and therefore there being more customer machines passing through the door, the three mechanics often found that they were looking for work to do, and even competing for the different jobs.

The three men and Katie sat down for lunch, each opening their individually wrapped sandwiches while the jug boiled.

Before he took a bite, Michael asked, 'When was the last time you were on eBay?'

The old mechanic thought a moment while he chewed and swallowed his food. 'Umm, prob'ly when we were lookin' for the parts to fix Kieran's Bonnie. So about three months ago. Why do you ask?'

'I think it might be time we started lookin' at gettin' another machine to restore.'

'D'ya have anythin' in mind?'

'Yeah, something cheap that we can make a fortune on!'

'Huh, dream on.'

'You're a Norton man Dad,' said Katie, 'how about getting one of those?'

'Actually, what I've always wanted to do is make a Triton – a Triumph 750 Bonneville motor in a Norton Featherbed frame. That way you don't have to make sure everything's authentic and true to the original. And you can make sensible improvements without having to worry about the "rivet counters".'

'But could we make any money on one?' posed Michael.

'I've seen well made Tritons goin' for $25k or more. The trick'll be to get the parts as cheaply as we can.'

'Where do ya get the parts for a Triton?' asked Paul who had never before heard of one, let alone seen or worked on one.

'The first place to look is eBay.'

The quartet was just finishing lunch when baby Kieran began squawking, announcing that it was time for his lunch as well. While Katie attended to his needs, a Police Divisional Van entered the laneway outside. Michael went out to investigate.

In the front seat were two Police Officers in uniform; Constable Tyler was driving and Senior Constable Robison was his passenger. Robison wound down his window as the van approached Michael.

'Doing your regular patrols?' asked Michael.

'Actually, we wanted to pass on some news that you might find comforting.'

'What's that?'

'A warrant for the arrest of Vincent Rogers has just been issued by the Tamworth Magistrate's Court. With any luck we'll catch him and he'll be off the streets quick smart and everyone'll be able to sleep soundly again.'

'That's great news. My father-in-law'll be rapt.'

'Don't get too excited. We haven't caught him yet.'

'But you will catch him.'

'Of course we will. Every spare resource is being thrown at this case to get it solved.'

Even though Vince Rogers and his gang of thieves had still been roaming the streets, the old mechanic's level of anxiety had lessened with the passing of time. It was now nearly two weeks since the gang had attacked the workshop with their Molotov cocktails. Nevertheless, the news that the Wheels of Justice were slowly turning in their favour gave everyone cause to celebrate.

For Paul, the news was bitter sweet. On the positive side it meant that he would be able to return to live under the same roof as the old mechanic, but conversely, eventually his role in the capture of Vince Rogers would be revealed, and everyone in the Tamworth Aboriginal and Torres Strait Islander Community would know. At least the change in his domestic circumstances would mean that he would be able to reassess his relationship with Grace. After all, how do you court someone you share a house with, especially when her grandparents shared the same space.

Paul had been quieter than his usual self as he pondered how to resolve his issues. Everything was so much more complicated living on the outside, compared to being in prison. In fact, when he was inside, all the big decisions were made for him – when to get up, when to go to bed, when to sleep, when to eat, when to work, what to wear. Even when he was in the gang, they decided everything for him. He just went along and did what they said. But on the outside, now that he had his freedom, he found that he had to make all the decisions himself, something that he was feeling less and less comfortable with each day. That evening, before he went to bed, he voiced his concerns to Uncle Danny.

'I'm scared.'

The Kamilaroi Elder listened.

'When I was on the inside, I couldn't wait to be released; I longed for me freedom. I wanted to decide for meself how to run me life. I was tired of everyone else tellin' me when to do this an' when to do that, how to live me life. But now I'm free, an' now I'm in control of me own decisions, I'm scared.'

'What're you scared for Paulie?'

'I'm scared I'll make the wrong choices; that I'll screw up.'

The Kamilaroi Elder smiled. 'Ah Paulie. Everyone makes wrong decisions, everyone chooses the wrong path, sometimes. The trick is to make sure you only chose the wrong way one time. And when you choose the wrong path, you learn for nex' time. You already choosed the right path more'n one time. I'm so proud of the wise decisions you keep makin', an' your mumma, she'd be proud too. It's good that you're scared of makin' wrong choices, 'cos then you'll be thinkin' before you make one.'

'What if I make the wrong choice but, even after I thought about it?'

Uncle Danny did not reply. There was no right or wrong answer, and no amount of wisdom could provide one.

Chapter 18

THE RECKONING

Locating a Norton Featherbed frame was proving a more difficult assignment than the old mechanic had first envisaged. Where once they were as common as dog's droppings, now they were as rare as the proverbial rocking horse poo. Of the four on eBay, three were located in the USA, while the other was in the UK. All were in various states of disrepair, but even the cheapest was in excess of a thousand dollars US, which did not include the costs of postage, packaging or taxes into Australia.

He had already rummaged through the pile of wrecked frames he had at the back of the workshop. There were a couple of Featherbed frames rusting away with all the other junk, but they were in such poor condition, they were not really worth salvaging. The only use that could be made was to weld that portion showing the frame number onto a newly made frame, but that would only be an option of last resort.

There was always the option of purchasing a new replica Featherbed frame, but the whole purpose of getting an original frame was that the resulting bike only had to pass the design standards current at the date of manufacture to get through registration. A bike made with a new frame, on the other hand, had to pass the much stricter present-day design standards. Furthermore, a replica frame was much more expensive than an original frame, even if it was made to a higher standard using more modern manufacturing methods and metallurgy.

On the off-chance, he called his mate old-Ned, with whom he had swapped a 1958 Wideline Featherbed frame for the 1959 frame for Michael's ES2 at the Gatton swap meet several years previously. The frame had cost him $200 on top of the one he had, but it was still a good buy. The good news was that old-Ned still had the frame, but that it would now cost him $750 plus postage and packaging. Still, it was cheaper than getting one from the States.

His initial choice of motor was a 1978-80 750cc Triumph Bonneville T140 with twin Amal carburettors and five-speed gearbox. But these motors had their oil tank in the frame and frequently suffered overheating problems due to their low oil capacity, even if that capacity could be increased by the use of an oil cooler.

As the engine size was dictated by the frame, the only requirement was that the motor had to be a twin of 500cc to 800cc capacity. If he was to use a 2007 790cc Triumph Thruxton twin motor, he would have a bike with a modern drive-train, electrics, fuelling and mechanical reliability, all while only having to register the bike as a 1958 Norton Dominator. The later motor was also cheaper and easier to source than a T140 motor. Indeed, he was able to purchase an entire wrecked bike for under a thousand dollars.

The Aboriginal and Torres Strait Islander Community in Tamworth was not an homogenous grouping of peoples, despite appearances. Like in the wider community, it was made up of a number of culturally diverse peoples each practicing their own religious beliefs and customs. While the Kamilaroi mob was by far the largest individual grouping, there were also sizeable numbers from the nearby Muruwari,

Kooma, Bigambul and Wailwan tribes, as well as a smattering of coastal Worimis and Awabakals from the Hunter.

Adding further to the complexity was that there had been much intermarriage between the various tribes and within the wider community. The resulting mix had vastly divergent views on their place in the community and the degree of cooperation that they were prepared to give to the various authorities and institutions. There were some who believed in living a quiet life within the wider Society, while there were others, often the more radical elements, who believed in a total separation of blacks and whites. So while Uncle Danny Stewart had a good deal of authority and respect within the Kamilaroi tribe in which he was an Elder, his influence was significantly less in some of the other mobs.

The consequence was that, when news emerged of the circumstances of the arrest of Vince Rogers, and the part that Paul Saunders and Daryl Porter, the other former gang member had played, there was a degree of disquiet in some, and complete outrage in others. In spite of the problems that Rogers had caused within and to the Aboriginal and Torres Strait Islander Community, some believed that he should have been dealt with within that same community. For Paul and Daryl to have given statements to the Police was seen by some as nothing short of a betrayal of their own people, beliefs, customs and culture.

The concept of "payback" as a part of Aboriginal tribal law, is seen by many in the wider Australian community as archaic, harsh and brutal, and is the area that often brings conflict between the Aboriginal and Torres Strait Islander Community and the civil authorities. In ages past, payback was delivered by the Elders of the community in order to keep members under control and to deliver punishment for crimes committed. But since the breakdown of cultural boundaries, some individual elements within the community used it to exact revenge on others that they determined had committed wrongs, whether perceived or real.

Both the old mechanic and Paul breathed a huge sigh of relief when they heard the television news reports that Vincent Rogers had been arrested. His capture was confirmed by a visit to the workshop on the following Monday by Senior Constable Robison and Constable Tyler.

'What happens now?' asked Paul.

'He'll be charged before he appears before the Magistrate,' advised the Senior Constable. 'With any luck he'll be remanded in custody until he's committed for trial.'

'What happens if he gets bail?' asked Michael.

'I doubt he'll get it; we'll certainly be opposing bail. But even if he does, he'll have to front up to the station daily and stay clean. Even if he farts, we'll know about it.'

'What protection does Paul receive if he does get bail?' asked Katie. 'He'll be sure to find out that the only reason he's been arrested is because of the statements that Paul and the other guy gave you.'

'I'm sure we won't need to provide any protection. But even in a worse case scenario, we can get an AVO taken out against Rogers.'

'AVO, huh! They're not worth the paper they're written on,' declared the old mechanic. 'Every week we hear of some poor woman murdered by a bloke who's broken an AVO.'

'Look, I don't think there's gonna be an issue. Rogers won't be getting bail, and none of you'll have anything to worry about.'

'Let's hope so.' The old mechanic turned to Paul. 'When you gonna move back?'

'Tomorra?'

'Sounds a plan!'

As it turned out, it was not Vince Rogers, or his gang, that anyone needed to be concerned about.

The first hint of unrest came a week prior to Christmas when Rogers' application for bail was formally refused and he was remanded in custody until a date to be fixed in the following February. A vocal minority of Aboriginal activists protested outside the Tamworth Magistrates Court that Vincent Rogers and his gang were victims of white prejudice and injustice and that they should be tried under Aboriginal tribal law. Naturally, the small group's argument was not given much credence, although a reporter from the local newspaper did write a couple of paragraphs about the matter to fill up space on page 12. Everyone else thought that it was high time the law had caught up with the gang leader and his cohorts.

With Rogers sent to the Silverwater Remand Centre in Sydney, the local activists realised that they needed to take a different approach to push their particular agenda. The small group was ignorant of the part that Uncle Danny Stewart had played in convincing Daryl Porter, Paul's former gang colleague, to give a statement to the Police. However, once the evidence had been provided to the solicitor defending Rogers, the names of both Paul and Daryl were out in the public domain. While the Police Prosecutor had applied for a suppression order of their names, the request was denied. With Porter still an inmate of Tamworth Correctional Centre, Paul became their main target.

The old mechanic had been slowly assembling the various parts he needed to construct the Triton. Besides the frame, and the motor and gearbox, he needed to get a fuel tank, seat unit, spoked wheels complete with brakes, new tyres, front and rear guards, a swingarm and a pair of front forks, as well as all the ancillaries. He would be able to fabricate the mounting plates to fit the motor and gearbox into the frame. He would also need to engineer the necessary spacers to ensure the drivetrain and the rear wheel sprockets aligned.

Ideally, he would use a pair of Norton Roadholder front forks as they would fit into the standard Norton triple clamps and headstock, and were the right width for standard Norton axles and twin leading shoe front brakes. However, just like Featherbed frames, Roadholder forks were getting harder to find. There were a few on eBay, but the vendors were asking extortionate prices.

The other option would be to repair the standard Triumph Thruxton forks and modify the Triumph triple clamps to be able to attach to the Norton headstock. That way, he would be able to have much more modern front suspension components, as well as disk brakes in lieu of the less efficient and effective twin-leading shoe drum brake set-up.

Locating a suitable fuel tank and seat unit was also proving a challenge. The badly damaged Triumph tank would not fit onto the Wideline Featherbed frame, even if it was repaired. Same with the seat. Past experience had taught him that replica Norton tanks out of India were vastly inferior to those from made in the UK or USA, even if they were significantly cheaper. He eventually found a fibreglass Manx fuel tank and seat for sale in Sydney's western suburbs for $250. The only drawback being that the new owner would not be able to use bio-fuels in the tank, but he did not think that would be a problem.

The four workers gathered for their first cuppa of the day. Katie was holding baby Kieran who was the centre of attention, gooing and giggling, much to the amusement of father and grandfather.

'What are you pair doin' next week?' asked the old mechanic.

'What's next week?' asked Michael.

'Umm, Christmas! Haven't you noticed all the decorations and advertising everywhere?'

'We're not going anywhere this year,' advised Katie. 'There're too many idiots on the road, too much traffic and prices for accommodation is way too high. We thought we'd stay home and take a break when the schools go back.'

'Smart thinkin'.'

'Whad're we doin?' asked Paul.

'We usually shut up shop between Christmas an' New Year. So, you can go for a holid'y if you want. Do you have any friends or family you wanna visit?'

'No, not really. You're the only friends I got. In fact, you're like me fam'ly too.'

'Well, you're more than welcome to stay here,' said the old mechanic. 'D'ya have plans for Christmas lunch?'

'Yeah, Uncle Danny's invited me over. Gracie an' her parents'll be there. I think he wants ta patch things up between us.'

'Good idea.'

'D'you wanna come over to our place for lunch Christmas day?' Michael asked the old mechanic.

'Of course, you *are* me fam'ly. Is ya mum gonna be there?'

'Nah, she wants us to go over ta her place for dinner.'

'That's a shame. No Christmas cheer for Michael then.'

'Actually, since I'm still breast feeding,' advised Katie, 'I'm also the designated driver.'

Michael's smile was like the cat who had just licked a bowl of cream.

The ringleader of the small band of Aboriginal activists wasted little time in locating where Paul Saunders lived and worked. Being on the extreme fringe of the Aboriginal Land Rights and Reconciliation movement, the actions of the group went largely unnoticed by most in the Tamworth Aboriginal and Torres Strait Islander Community, let alone the Police. Those who were aware, dismissed them out of hand.

The four workers were completely unaware that the activists had already driven down the laneway between the workshop and the small cottage late at night. But where the gang had been bent on destroying the place where Paul worked, they, on the other hand were determined to send a personal message to the Aboriginal mechanic, and indeed to the wider community. No-one else needed to get hurt, unless of course they got in the way.

The weather had been fine in the lead-up to Christmas, with hot sunny days and warm nights. Unlike in the Northern Hemisphere, Christmas was nearly always hot in Australia and meals tended to reflect the warmer weather — salads and seafood. The storm season had abated and the farmland crops were growing steadily under the bright summer sunshine.

Three days prior to Christmas, the small band of activists arrived about midnight in two cars that they parked at the end of the laneway. There were six Aboriginal men, two armed with spears, two with clubs or nulla nullas and two with dry bark kindling and fire sticks. They were each almost naked with small red cloths tied around their waists and white ochre paint on their faces and bodies. In the darkness, they were almost invisible.

They built a small fire in the backyard of the cottage and started singing quietly. As the flames grew in strength, so the volume of their voices rose. Paul awoke to the noise. He looked from his bedroom window and saw the fire, but he only noticed one of the men.

He crept from his bed. The old mechanic was still asleep. Dressed only in his shorts, he opened the kitchen door and stepped outside. Two of the activists were waiting for him. Standing either side of the door, they grabbed him from behind and held his arms tightly. He cried out. Paul struggled, but the two men were strong and held him easily. They dragged him toward the fire.

'Let me go,' cried Paul, 'I ain't done nothin'. Let me go!'

The more he struggled, the tighter he was held.

The ringleader of the activists raised his voice. 'Paul Saunders, for betraying your own people, beliefs and culture, and giving support to the enemy, you have been sentenced to a spearing.'

'He's done nothin' of the sort,' called the old mechanic from the back door.

'This has nothin' ta do with you ol' man. This is payback; black fella justice.'

'Justice, my eye. Leave him alone.'

Two of the other activists quickly surrounded him. One raised his club and landed a blow on the back of his head, immediately knocking him out cold. He fell down in a crumpled heap on the ramp.

The two men holding Paul, stretched his arms out so that he would be an easy target. After more singing, the ringleader raised his spear and threw it at Paul's right leg where it embedded itself in his upper thigh. He let out a cry in agony. He too would have collapsed to the ground if he had not been held up by the others. The second spear thrower hurled his spear at Paul's left leg. This one was not so well aimed and glanced off his shin, slicing through the inside of his calf muscle.

With the sentence carried out, Paul was freed. He dropped to the ground, his legs a bloody mess. The activists gathered their weapons and escaped as quietly as they had arrived. When news of the attack emerged, everyone in the Tamworth Aboriginal and Torres Strait Islander Community would know not to consort with the enemy.

AVO – Apprehended Violence Order

Chapter 19

CLEARING UP THE MESS

Paul knew that he was losing a lot of blood. While the two spears had missed all the major blood vessels in his legs, the two gaping wounds were still oozing copious amounts of the dark red fluid. With only a pair of shorts on, he needed to get into the house and find something to staunch the flow.

The old mechanic had not moved since he had fallen after being bludgeoned on the back of his head. Paul did not even know if he was still alive. But he needed to help himself before he could come to the other man's aid. He stripped off his shorts and tied the garment tightly around his calf. Then, placing the heel of his palm over the puncture wound in his thigh, he tried to stand.

The pain was excruciating, particularly the deep puncture wound. He tried taking his mind off his injuries. He cast his mind back to another time when he was in a lot of pain. During his initiation ceremony, he had almost passed out when he was circumcised with the flint knife in prison. He clenched his teeth and stood. Tears dampened his eyes.

The night was quiet. The only noises were from the crickets in the garden and cicadas in the trees. There were no other sounds except his own muffled whimpers as he made his way slowly up the ramp to the cottage. He felt giddy from the loss of blood.

As he edged past the old mechanic, he bent down to check for a pulse. While the older man was laying awkwardly, he was breathing and his heart was beating strongly. There was blood on the back of his head and more on the ramp, but Paul knew he could do little for him as he was, so he moved on. With each step, he left a trail of bloody footprints into the kitchen where he called the emergency number. He sat naked at the kitchen table, waiting for help to arrive.

The Emergency Services rushed to the address. Senior Constable Robison and Constable Tyler were working the night shift in the next suburb. When they heard the address on the radio, they knew that somehow their star witness was in trouble. But it was not until much later in the hospital and saw for themselves the injuries to Paul's legs that they realised just how much trouble that was.

The Police arrived at the cottage just as the second ambulance was leaving to take the old mechanic to the hospital. Apart from the blood and the dying embers of the fire, there was little to reveal what had occurred. They called for a guard to be placed at the cottage and another at the hospital.

When Michael and Katie arrived at the workshop with baby Kieran the next morning, they were surprised to see Police officers swarming the area. Their car was prevented from entering the laneway; Police tape barred the way while a young Constable stopped the car.

'What's going on?' asked Michael.

'Who are you?'

'Mike Jones, and my wife Katie. We work here. What's happened?'

'I'm afraid there's been an incident.'

'What kind of incident?'

'Has something happened to my father?' asked Katie, a knot in her stomach, already starting to fear the worst.

'Two men have been assaulted. They've both been taken to Tamworth Base Hospital. I'm afraid I'm not at liberty to tell you any more than that.'

'Oh no, not again, not now. Mikey, quickly, let's get to the hospital.'

The trio found the old mechanic in the Emergency Department having his head stitched and bandaged. An x-ray had already revealed that there were no skull fractures, but he was severely concussed. He was tired and groggy, and still in his pyjamas.

'Daddy, are you okay?' asked Katie, almost in tears. 'What happened?'

'Hello sweetheart. Yeah, I think I'm awright, but I've got a stinkin' headache.'

'Where's Paul?' asked Michael.

'I don't know.'

'Did he do this to you?'

The old mechanic seemed confused and distressed as he tried to recall the events of the previous evening. 'I don't remember.'

Michael looked around. He spied Constable Tyler speaking with the Emergency Department Doctor and headed in his direction.

When the two had finished talking, Michael, pointing toward the old mechanic, asked, 'What happened to my father-in-law?'

The doctor replied, 'He received a blow to the head, but other than a severe concussion and some stitches, he'll be okay.'

He then left the pair to attend to other patients.

'Do you know what happened?' asked Michael.

'Things're a bit sketchy at the moment,' Constable Tyler replied, 'but it appears the old guy surprised some black fellas giving Paul some rough justice for speaking to us.'

'Didn't we tell you he needed protection? Where's Paul now?'

'He's in theatre getting stitched up.'

'What happened to him?'

'His legs got sliced up pretty bad. It looks like he got a couple wounds from a knife or a machete or something. He lost a fair amount of blood. We haven't had much of a chance to speak with him yet.'

'Well, there's no point askin' George anythin'. I don't think he even knows what day it is.'

'We'll drop by to see him in a coupla days then.'

When the old mechanic had been cleared to leave, Michael and Katie took him home. By the time they arrived, the Police Forensic Team had been and gone. They had taken samples of the spilled blood on the ramp, in the yard and inside the cottage for DNA matching. They also found a number of smudged finger-prints on the railing and door handle, but whether they belonged to the victims or the perpetrators was yet to be determined.

A number of customers had arrived at the workshop to have their motorcycles repaired or serviced, only to be turned away by the Police. There would be no work today.

A young female Police Constable had just locked the kitchen door when Michael and Katie pulled up in the laneway.

'Can we go in now?' asked Michael.

'Yeah, but I've just locked the door,' replied the Constable.

'That's alright; we've got a key.'

'There's a lot of blood on the floor.'

'There's a lot of blood everywhere.'

Michael helped the old mechanic to bed while Katie brought baby Kieran into the cottage, before they both started cleaning up the mess. They were appalled at the amount of blood everywhere. Paul's bloody footprints were starting to bake in the warm mid-morning sunshine. The timber slats on the ramp would need to be scrubbed with a hard brush and blasted with a gurney to remove the stains.

Neither of them wanted to think about what had happened the previous night, let alone the consequences for the future. While they were concerned for Paul and his injuries, they were more worried about the old mechanic, that he had been put in danger for no fault of his own. But their immediate concern was to clean up the mess.

News of the attack spread quickly within the Tamworth Aboriginal and Torres Strait Islander Community. Some, an insignificant minority, believed that Paul had got what he deserved, while the rest were outraged. They believed, quite rightly, that the actions of a few extremists on the fringes reflected poorly on the entire community. Even those who believed Paul was wrong in giving a statement to the Police believed the extremists had gone too far.

Uncle Danny Stewart had heard from the PALO, who had been informed by Senior Constable Robison. The Kamilaroi Elder went straight to the hospital to see Paul. Grace tagged along with him. They found him in the recovery ward tethered to a drip and a machine checking his vital signs.

The Elder felt great sympathy and compassion for his young protégé as he lay in the bed on the edge of consciousness. He somehow felt responsible for what had occurred the previous night, even if he was not exactly sure of all the details. But he was fairly certain he knew who was responsible, even if he could not prove it. Grace started weeping when she saw her man connected to the machines. She grasped his hand. He squeezed hers in reply.

'You awake Paulie?' asked Uncle Danny.

His eyes fluttered open briefly, but he did not say anything.

'Do ya know who done this to ya?'

He shook his head and croaked, 'No.'

'You sleep Paulie. We'll find 'em; we'll find 'em and stop 'em.'

Leaving Grace to keep vigil at the young Aboriginal mechanic's bedside, Uncle Danny left the hospital. On the outside he was his normal calm and genial self, but inwardly he was raging. For years he had been working hard for Aboriginal Reconciliation, bringing together the black and white communities, teaching both sides that Aboriginal culture and beliefs needed to be acknowledged and respected. But it seemed that every time he took a step forward, a small group of people just kept dragging him back. The frustrating thing for him was that these were the same people who had most to gain from his work. But this was a fight he would not lose; indeed, he was determined not to.

Paul was released from hospital into the care of Uncle Danny Stewart on Christmas eve. The Police had taken statements from both the old mechanic and Paul, but neither could tell them much more than they had gleaned from the evidence at the scene. Paul had no idea who the men were who had attacked him, while the old mechanic could hardly remember anything at all. While the physical wounds would heal in time, the mental scars would remain.

Paul was keen to see the old mechanic, so he asked Uncle Danny to drop by at the cottage before taking him home. It would also be an opportunity for him to pick up some of his belongings.

Using crutches to get about, Paul's legs were bound tightly to protect the numerous stitches in his left calf and right thigh. He hobbled up to the back screen-door; the Kamilaroi Elder behind him. The old mechanic was making tea.

'Hey Paul, Uncle Danny, how ya doin'?'

'Hey George, they jus' let me out.'

Uncle Danny waved hello before opening the door for Paul.

'You're just in time for a cuppa.'

The old mechanic made tea for Uncle Danny and himself and a coffee for Paul. When they were all seated at the kitchen table, the young Aboriginal mechanic spoke.

'I'm sorry George.'

'Sorry, for what?'

'Fer gettin' ya inta this mess.'

'Look Paul, you weren't responsible for what happened the other night.'

'They were my mob what hit you but.'

'Hey, if everyone took the blame for everything done by their own people, then I'm just as responsible. There's no way we could've foreseen what would've happened when you gave that statement to the Police.'

'If I hadn't gone to the cops but, none of this woulda happened.'

'Paul, I think you've forgotten why you gave the statement. Vince Rogers is a crook who needed to be stopped. He tried to burn down the workshop if you recall.'

'Yeah, if I'd jus' gone wiff him but, you woulda been safe.'

'Yeah, but what about the rest of Tamworth. Rogers' is nothin' but an oxygen thief, an' so were the people who attacked us the other night. Paul, you don't have to apologise for doing what needed to be done. You did the right thing. Okay?'

'Thanks George.'

The two men embraced. Uncle Danny smiled.

'Now, how're your legs?'

'Sore. How's ya head?'

'Yeah, sore. When do ya get the stitches out?'

Paul shrugged his shoulders. 'I gotta get the bandages changed every coupla days. Grace says she wants ta be me nurse.'

'Half ya luck.'

'They're worried about infections, so I'm on some pretty strong antibiotics.'

'Do the cops have any idea who did it yet?'

'We know who done it,' Uncle Danny replied. 'They won't do it again.'

The statement was half promise, half threat. The old mechanic knew that the Kamilaroi Elder meant what he said.

While Paul made his way to his bedroom to gather his belongings, Uncle Danny talked with the old mechanic.

'We'll look after Paulie fer a coupla weeks, 'til 'e c'n start workin' ag'in.'

'That's fine, the workshop's closed until after the New Year. He prob'ly needs a holid'y anyway.'

'All our mob are very proud of Paulie, fer what 'e's done.'

'You have every right to be.'

'We also wanna thank you and the two youngens fer helpin' 'im make the move from prison ta bein' a useful member o' the community.'

'That's alright. Paul made it easy for us.'

Paul caught the tail end of the conversation. 'What made it easy?'

'Nothin'. We're talkin' aboucha, not to ya.'

Paul was confused while the older pair laughed.

Chapter 20

PLAYING SANTA CLAUS

Christmas morning dawned unseasonably cool. Despite the festive season occurring during the summer months in the Southern Hemisphere, very occasionally we experience a white Christmas, even if it is more likely from a hail storm rather than from a dumping of snow. After weeks of hot dry weather, a change in the early hours of the morning brought scattered showers and cool south-westerly winds.

Many Australian families have long ago dispensed with the traditional Christmas fare of roast turkey and hams, having made the switch to cold meat salads and seafood, with fresh lobsters, prawns, oysters, fish, crabs, mussels, scallops and Moreton Bay bugs jockeying for space on the dining table. Nevertheless, there are some stalwarts who consider that Christmas is not really Christmas without the Christmas roast.

In their busy lives, Michael and Katie do not usually have the time to spend in the kitchen roasting a large piece of meat, whether that be a leg of lamb or a side of beef, let alone a whole turkey, not that they have a particular yearning for any of these meats. They are not even very fussed about roast chicken or baked ham.

When Christmas day rolls around, they always make a special effort to cook their favourite roast meat: pork belly. Of course, that means more than just roasting a piece of belly pork, because it includes crackling, and apple sauce, and gravy, and roast vegies, as well as the traditional plum pudding soaked in whisky covered in hot brandy custard, with a dollop of fresh whipped cream on top. So, a cooler Christmas day than usual, just made it much more pleasant for the family to cook what they had planned for the day anyway.

For some people, Christmas day is one of the most important days on the religious calendar, probably second only to Easter. But for the majority of Australians, Christmas day is all about families, coming together to share a meal and to exchange gifts; it certainly was for the old mechanic. Since his wife had died from breast cancer, and he had suffered his heart attack, he had made a determined effort to be there for Michael, Katie and baby Kieran; not just helping to make the business run successfully, but also ensuring that any difficulties, be they financial, technical or relational, were resolved before they could cause any lasting problems.

The old mechanic heard, rather than felt the change in the weather. The rain had been pattering on the corrugated iron roof of his cottage since about 3:00 am; a sound he found comforting rather than annoying. Even though it was Christmas morning, and he had no reason to get up early, he was a creature of habit and had set the alarm to wake himself at 6:00. He dozed in the darkness while he waited for the time to elapse. When it did, he turned the alarm off and headed for the bathroom to shave.

Not being one for large or extravagant gifts, the old mechanic made every effort to find something personal that each person would want and cherish. For Katie, he found a silver bracelet that included the birth stones of her parents, her husband, her son and herself. For Michael, it was a Swiss made automatic chronograph with a tachymeter to show elapsed time and average speed. For baby Kieran, being his first Christmas, it was a hand-made wooden rocking motorcycle. While he was still too young to ride the bike, grandfather knew he would grow into it. Dressed in his Sunday best, and with the gifts wrapped and stowed into the cabin of his truck, he headed off to Banjo Creek around mid-morning. It was time to play Santa Claus.

Just as for the old mechanic, Christmas day in Uncle Danny's household was all about family. The only difference being that Grace felt obligated to attend the Christmas day church service with her parents. While she no longer considered herself to be a "believer" as such, she did not want to cause offence, particularly on such an important occasion. Besides which, she loved singing Christmas carols, both traditional and modern, so this was a time that she was able to exercise her vocal cords, as well as making her parents happy.

The bandages on Paul's legs meant that his mobility was severely restricted, made worse by the fact that he did not have a licence to drive a car. With the injuries to his lower limbs limiting his ability to ride a motorcycle, not to mention the fact he was still in a significant amount of pain, he was now totally dependent on others for transport. He would have liked to attend the Christmas day church service with Grace, but decided against it, as her parents were still not particularly happy about their relationship. He hoped that things would change with the intervention of Uncle Danny.

The Kamilaroi Elder had planned to barbecue a suckling pig, Aboriginal style. This meant a whole stuffed animal wrapped in paperbark and cooked in the ground under the coals of a fire. Traditionally, the animal would have been a kangaroo or a wallaby, or maybe even a wombat, but to locate one suitable for human consumption was now a very difficult proposition, especially as some native animals were protected by law. However, the inclement weather forced a change of plans. The alternate method involved a 44-gallon drum cut in half, filled with burning charcoal over a grate and a makeshift rotisserie that required someone to keep the meat turning. To ensure the rain did not douse the fire, the barbecue was moved to a corrugated iron lean-to off the garage.

Paul watched as Uncle Danny lit the fire using dry kindling. Once the flames died down, he fed the fire with pieces of charcoal. Charcoal is used in preference to wood as it burns evenly with more heat, but less flames, and importantly, less smoke. Auntie Dot had prepared the suckling pig, filling the cavity with a mixture of fresh chopped fruits, dried fruits and nuts, and spices before sewing it up with twine and having it skewered. The young Aboriginal volunteered to keep the meat turning to ensure it cooked evenly and did not burn, a job he could do sitting down.

As he kept the rotisserie turning, he thought about his life, and how it had turned. Where once he had considered the gang as his "band of brothers". He realised that he now had three families: there were his blood relatives, his sisters and one day he hoped, Grace; there was his family through his initiation, Uncle Danny, Aunty Dot and the other Kamilaroi Elders and tribe members; and there were his work colleagues, who were also his friends.

Paul did not feel any animosity toward the people who had speared him earlier in the week. He understood the concept of payback, but whether they were right or wrong to subject him to that particular traditional law, he would leave to the Elders to determine. He took comfort from Uncle Danny's declaration that that would be the end; no further action would be taken. He felt the same way. Even if the police caught the perpetrators, he decided that he would not testify against them. Justice had been served.

Grace returned from church with her parents just before midday. She changed out of her dress into jeans and joined Paul outside.

'How was church?' he asked.

'Yeah, it was alright. We sang lotsa Christmas songs. It woulda been better if you'd come with us but. How're your legs?'

'They feel better in front o' this fire. Did ya mum 'n dad come back wiff ya?'

'Yeah, they're inside takin' ta grandma 'n grandad.'

'What about?'

'Us, I think.'

Paul did not speak for some minutes as he thought about his life.

Eventually he said, 'If your mum 'n dad are okay about it, do ya wanna get married?'

Grace squealed with delight. 'Oh yes please.'

She threw her arms around Paul, almost knocking him off his chair, before giving him a long passionate kiss on the lips.

When she came up for air, Paul said, 'Merry Christmas Gracie.'

'Merry Christmas to you too Paulie. I love you.'

'I love ya too.'

The old mechanic parked his truck and approached Katie and Michael's Unit. He knocked at the door which was decorated with a wreath of mistletoe and bells, and a sign that wished a Merry Christmas to All. As he waited, he could hear music from inside the Unit; Michael Bublé was crooning *It's Beginning to Look a Lot Like Christmas*. The old mechanic mused, yep, it sure is.

The music was turned down before Katie opened the door. 'Hi Daddy, Merry Christmas!'

'Merry Christmas to you too, Sweetheart.'

Katie gave her father a kiss and a hug. He had his arms full, so he could only respond by kissing her in return. He placed the gifts under the Christmas tree and picked up baby Kieran who was in his bouncinette.

'Hello Little Man, Merry Christmas to you too.'

Kieran gooed in a dribbly reply.

'Hi George,' called Michael from the kitchenette, 'Merry Christmas.'

'Same to you Mike.'

'There's a beer in the fridge, or you can open a bottle of wine if you like. There's also some egg-nog if you'd prefer?'

'It's a bit early for alcohol. But I'll have a cuppa if that's okay?'

'I'll make you one,' volunteered Katie.

'Thanks Sweetheart.'

The small dining table had been laid out with their "special occasion" *Mikasa* dinner set and silver cutlery set, crystal wine glasses, Christmas serviettes and bonbons, candles and gravy boat. The old mechanic recognised the dinner set as the one his wife had given to Katie when she first left home. That seemed such a long time ago now.

Sitting down at the breakfast bar with his mug of tea, the old mechanic said, 'Mm, somethin' smells nice.'

'I hope you like pork,' replied Michael.

'Sorry Mike, I don't.'

Michael looked at his father-in-law in alarm.

The old mechanic smiled. 'I don't like pork; I love it … just as long as there's cracklin' and apple sauce.'

Michael gave a relieved sigh. 'Is there any other way to have it?'

'Yeah, but I don't like it the other way.'

'I'll keep that in mind.'

'How's your head Dad?' asked Katie.

'Yeah, it's fine now. It's still a bit tender to the touch. I get the stiches out nex' week.'

'Have the cops caught the people who did it yet?'

'I haven't heard. But I got a visit yesterd'y. Uncle Danny dropped in with Paul. He got discharged from the hospital. He's stayin' with the ol' fella over the Chrissy break.'

'What are we gonna do with Paul?' asked Michael.

'Whaddya mean?'

'Well,' said Katie, 'it's because of Paul that the workshop nearly got torched …'

'And you got assaulted and ended up in hospital,' continued Michael.

'Hey, come on you two,' pleaded the old mechanic, 'Paul wasn't responsible for the fire or the assault, and remember, he came out worse than anyone from all this.'

'Dad, just because it's Christmas, doesn't mean you have to play Santa Claus,' said Katie. 'Sure, Paul wasn't directly responsible for the fire or the assault, but he was indirectly responsible. If he wasn't involved with that gang and if he wasn't an Aboriginal, none of this would've happened.'

'Yeah, if he didn't have all that baggage to begin with,' added Michael, 'we wouldn't be in the mess we're in now.'

'Come on Katie, Mike, that's not fair. That's like sayin' if I didn't live in Tamworth, or if I didn't ride a motorbike, none of this would've happened. We can't change who we are or what we do, an' we can't change the events that shape us. Everyone has baggage, even you two. We can't change the past, but we can do somethin' about the future.

'Paul's had a tough life right from the beginnin'. He started behind just by being born a black fella. He's faced discrimination his whole life. Yeah, he fell in with the wrong crowd, but everyone makes at least one mistake in life. Should that hold him back forever? We were the first white fellas to give him a break – his first job and somewhere safe ta live. Is it right that we turn our backs on him now, just 'cos things are gettin' a bit uncomf'table for us?'

No-one spoke, so he continued.

'Do you remember when you first came ta me Mike? You had no job, no money and a bike that wasn't runnin' real flash. You had baggage too: your ol' man, and you'd been bullied at the place you us'ta work. But I gave you a break. I saw your potential. Now, you're runnin' the show, you married me daughter, you've got a car, a bike a house, an' a child of your own. Was I playin' Santa Claus then? But you started streets ahead of where Paul was.

'Y'know, when Paul dropped in to see me yesterd'y, he apologised for the actions of those black fellas who hit me. The reason he did so was 'cause they were his own people. But at the end of the day, he got hurt, and I got hurt, because someone decided enough was enough. Paul did the right thing by standin' up to the gang, refusin' to join up with 'em again, and he did the right thing by givin' the police the statement that put that bastard gang leader in prison. An' I'm gonna do the right thing by standin' up for him, whatever the consequences.'

There was silence in the room for a few minutes. Katie had tears in her eyes. Michael turned away in shame.

'I'm sorry Daddy, I didn't think,' said Katie at last. 'I was really only concerned for you and your safety.'

'That's alright Sweetheart, I know you are.'

'Yeah, I'm sorry too George,' said Michael.

'That's all right. You know a wise man once said, "The only thing necessary for the triumph of evil is for good men to do nothing." Paul did the right thing by givin' that statement to the cops, and I think that by standin' by him and supportin' him, we're doin' the right thing too.'

* "The only thing necessary for the triumph of evil is for good men to do nothing." Possibly attributed to philosopher Edmund Burke.
 https://en.wikiquote.org/wiki/Edmund_Burke

Epilogue

Paul and Grace were married on the Australia Day long weekend in a traditional ceremony. While many Aboriginal Australians see Australia Day as "Invasion Day", the day that commemorates the beginning of white settlement of mainland Australia, they chose that day specifically to redefine it as a Day of Reconciliation and respect.

On a personal level, there was the reconciliation of Paul and Grace with her parents, and the respect that both parents and children had for each other. While Grace's parents were still unhappy that she had turned her back on her belief in God, they respected her right to do so, even though they continued to pray for the young couple.

On a wider perspective, Paul wanted to point to his reconciliation with members of the wider Tamworth Community. Where once he had been at enmity with the Police and the Judiciary, and had no respect for them, he was now a law abiding and contributing member of that same community.

Of course, Paul could not have reached this point in his life without the help and support of both the wider Aboriginal and Torres Strait Islander Community through Uncle Danny and Aunty Dot, as well as individuals within the White Community; specifically, Brian Redmond, the Prison Welfare Officer, Bob Petersen, his Parole Officer, the old mechanic, Michael and Katie.

Paul had earned the respect of those in the prison, and those with whom he worked, because of his desire to reform his life and make a clean break with his past, and because he wanted to break the cycle of crime and subsequent imprisonment that he found himself in. And with the respect he had earned, he was able to bring together, to reconcile both black fellas and white fellas.

With their savings and with help from the Aboriginal Housing Office in Tamworth and her parents, Paul and Grace were able to purchase a small cottage on the highway about two doors from the sandwich shop and 450 metres from the old workshop. They became friends with the shop owner, and were his regular customers. Paul was able to walk to work while Grace caught the bus to her office job in Tamworth. In time they had children of their own, twins – a boy and girl.

In time, he too was made an elder of the Kamilaroi mob, and he used his position in the workshop to mentor troubled young Aboriginals. He would train a succession of mechanics in the specifics of classic British motorcycles.

On baby Kieran's first birthday, Katie found out she was pregnant, this time she would have a girl. With their growing family, Katie and Michael decided to use the equity in their Unit to pay for a deposit on a four-bedroom house in a new estate in Banjo Creek, two streets away from where they had been living. They would then be able to keep the Unit as an investment property.

The old mechanic continued working for a while, but a series of minor strokes the following year meant that he had to spend time recovering. He had completed the Triton, although he had to wait several months for a buyer prepared to pay the asking price. But due to his poor health, and being no longer able to kick-start a bike for health reasons or ride due to balance issues, he decided to also sell his beloved Norton Dominator 99 SS. Michael would have wanted to keep his father-in-law's Norton, but he was already financially committed, so it went.

Vincent Rogers was eventually released from Long Bay Correctional Centre. But no sooner was he back on the streets, but he started using heroine and crystal meth amphetamine. He died three months later from an overdose. Nobody mourned his passing, least of all Paul Saunders.

THE END

Printed in Great Britain
by Amazon